PACKAGES

PACKAGES

STORIES BY RICHARD STERN

Coward, McCann & Geoghegan
New York

Stories in this collection appeared in *The Atlantic, Chicago, Commentary, Encounter, Harper's* and *TriQuarterly*.

"There came a wind like a bugle" by Emily Dickinson reprinted by permission of the publishers from *The Poems of Emily Dickinson*, edited by Thomas H. Johnson, Cambridge, MA: The Belknap Press of Harvard University Press, Copyright © 1951, 1955, 1979 by the President and Fellows of Harvard College.

Library of Congress Cataloging in Publication Data

Stern, Richard G, date
    Packages
    I. Title.
PZ4.S83943Pac   [PS3569.T39]   813'.54   80-13200
    ISBN 0-698-11041-2

Printed in the United States of America

For Saul and Philip, who've been here.

CONTENTS

PACKAGES

Wissler Remembers

Miss Fennig. Mr. Quincy. Mr. Parcannis. Miss Shimbel. Ms. Bainbridge. (Antique, silver-glassed, turn-of-the-century-Rebecca-West face; at 22.) Miss Vibsayana, who speaks so beautifully. (You cannot relinquish a sentence, the act of speech such honey in your throat, I can neither bear nor stop it.) Miss Glennie, Mr. Waldemeister. All of you.

Do you know what it is for me to see you here? To have you in this room three hours a week? Can you guess how I've grown to love you? How hard it is for me to lose you?

Never again will you be a group. (Odds against, trillions to one.) We've been together thirty hours, here in this room whose gaseous cylinders emend the erratic window light. Those spritzes of autumn the neo-Venetian neo-Gothic windows admit. We have spoken in this room of Abbot Suger, Minister of State, Inventor of Gothic, have cited his "Dull minds ascend through material things." (Not you, never yours.) But did I tell you that I took a trolley to his church, Saint Denis, sitting next to a Croatian lady who trembled when I told her that just a week before I'd talked with the little salesman Peter who'd been, who was, her king? There's been so much to tell you, woven by my peripatetic memory to our subject.

The thing is I want to tell you everything.

Though I will see some of you again, will write many of you letters of recommendation—for years to come—may even, God knows, teach your children (if you have them soon), may, some day, in Tulsa or West Hartford, see you when your present beauty is long gone, I know that what counts for us is over. When you come up to me in Oklahoma or Connecticut and ask if I remember you: "I took your Studies in Narrative course nine years ago"—or twenty-five—I will not remember. If you remind me that you wrote a paper on Wolfram's *Parzival*, that you were in class with the beautiful Indian girl, Miss was-it Bisayana? and Mr. Parcannis, the boy who leashed his beagle to his bicycle, perhaps I will make out through the coarsened augmentation and subtraction of the years both you and that beautiful whole that was the class of Autumn Seventy-Seven, Winter Sixty-Two. But what counts is gone.

Teaching.

I have been teaching classes for thirty years. Age twenty-one, I had a Fulbright Grant to teach fifteen hours a week at the Collège Jules Ferry in Versailles. The boys, *in-* and-*externes*, ages ten to nineteen, prepared for the baccalaureate exam. Four days a week, I walked the block and a half from the Pension Marie Antoinette and did my poor stuff. I was so ignorant of French, I had addressed the director as *Directoire*. ("I thought you were trying to get to a government bureau.") When I entered the classroom, the boys rose. A thrill and an embarrassment to an awkward fellow not born a prince of the blood. "Good morning, boys." "Good morning, Meestair Weeslair." Much sweetly wicked *ritardandi* of those long syllables. "Today we will do an American poem. I'll supply the French translation, you translate into English. Anyone who gets within twelve words of the original gets a present." Five of the twenty-five understand; they whisper explanation to the others. Blue, black, brown, gray, green eyes intensify and shimmer with competitive greed. (Every student is numbered by class standing and introduces himself accordingly: "I'm LeQuillec, sixteenth of twenty-five.") "Here's the poem. Forgive my pronunciation.

> *A qui sont les bois, je crois le savoir,*
> *Il a sa maison au village.*
> *Et si je m'arrête, il ne peut me voir,*
> *Guêttant ses bois qu'emplit la neige."*

The next day I collect the English versions.

> To whom are that wood, I believe to know it.
> It have its house at the village.
> And if I arrest, it is not able to see me,
> Staring its woods who fills the snow.

"Not first rate, LeQuillec. *Pas fort bien."* I read them the original. *"Ça vous plaît?"* Ah ouiiii, M. *Weeslairrre. Beaucoup!"*

I see LeQuillec's dark pout, the freckles of Strethmann, the begloved, elegant what's-his-name? Persec? Parsec? who wrote me the next year in Heidelberg. "Dear Mr.

Richard Stern

Wissler. How are you? I am well. You shall be happy to know I am fourteen of thirty-one this trimestre. How do you find Germany?"

Très bien, Persec. I am teaching at the University here. In the *Anglistikabteilung.* Two classes. For the *Ohrgeld,* four hundred marks—a hundred dollars—a semester. Not a great fortune, so I work for the Department of the Army decoding cables at the Staff Message Control. I have Top Secret clearance which enables me to forward the reports of suspected Russian breakthroughs at the Fulda Gap the coming Christmas Day. One week I work from six P.M. to two A.M., the next a normal daytime shift. My classes adjust to this schedule. *The American Literary Experience.* 1. *Prose.* 2. *Poetry.* The first assignment, James's *The Ambassadors.* American libraries all over West Germany send me their copies of the book. I give the class a week to read it. The class shrinks from forty to seven. I don't understand, they rapped on their desks for two minutes after Lecture One. Still, even students who apologize for dropping "because of schedule conflicts" come to me on the street, doff caps, shake hands. A girl runs up the Hauptstrasse to me, asks if I will sign a petition. "For Helgoland, Professor." "Fräulein . . ." "Hochhusen, Professor." She is nearly as tall as I, has hair a little like Ms. Bainbridge's, heart-rending popped blue eyes, hypnotic lips. "Forgive me, Fräulein, I don't think I can sign political petitions when I work for the American Army." Unlike students later on, she says, "I understand, Professor." What a smile. "Excuse me for troubling you." "No trouble, Fräulein. It's a pleasure to see you. I love you." (I do not say the last three words aloud.)

I teach the sons and daughters of soldiers whose bones have been left in the Ukraine and the Ardennes. I teach

14

Wissler Remembers

those who themselves fired guns, were prisoners, who
received lessons on such scum as I. We read Emily
Dickinson, Thoreau, *Benito Cereno*, Hawthorne (some of
whose nastier views run parallel to their old ones). I talk of
the power of blackness and try and connect it to the rubble
of Mannheim, Ludwigshafen, Frankfurt.

The first poems we do are German: Goethe, Trakl,
Heine. To show them what close reading can do for poems.
They take to such naked delights like literary sailors ashore
after months. *Sie sassen und tranken am Teetisch, Und sprachen
von Liebe viel.*

American soldiers fill the Heidelberg streets, eat in
special restaurants with special money. I live in a special
hotel, buy food in the American Commissary. *The ambassadors.*

Fräulein Hochhusen helps me with my first German
poem. "Will you check this for me, please, Fräulein? I just
felt like writing it. I don't trust my German at all."

> *Wir waren einmal ganz neu.*
> *Solange die Stellen brennen,*
> *brennen wir Heu.*

> Once we were utterly new.
> So long as places burn
> we burn [make?] hay.

"It is not exactly correct, Professor, but very, how shall I
say? *Eindrucksvoll. Original.* Original. And your German is
beautiful, Professor."

No, Fräulein, berry-cheeked Fräulein with the burnt hay
hair, it's you who are beautiful. Give me the petition,
darling Fräulein. Tell me about Helgoland. Will they test

15

bombs there? And who owns it? Germany? Denmark? I want to know everything. Is my poem true German? Is it a poem? Do you love me as I love you? "You're much too generous, Fräulein. I feel so bad about the petition."

Herr Doppelgut, stooped, paper-white, dog-eyed, had walked three hundred kilometers, "black across the border," yet manages to get whitely back to see his mother and bring me dirt-cheap books from East Berlin. When I go there Christmastime, with my visa stamped by all four occupying powers, I walk through thirty ex-blocks of ex-houses and ex-stores. Ash, stone dreck, half an arch, a pot, a toilet seat, a bicycle wheel, grimacing iron struts. Insane survivals. In front of the Russian memorial tank, a young guard holds a machine gun. From my new language text, I ask, *"Vy govoritny russki?"* Silence. *"Nyet?"* I think I see the muzzle waver. "Robot," I say; yards off. Gray ladies in beaten slippers fill carts with rubble and push them on tracks across the street where other aged ladies unload them. I go back to Thoreau's beans, to the white whale, to intoxicated bees and Alfred Prufrock; to Herr Doppelgut and Fräulein Hochhusen, to close readings of poems. Of breasts.

Yes, I cannot omit something important. In every class, there is another system of love at work. The necks, the ears, the breasts, the cropped hair of Ms. Bainbridge, the go-ahead green eyes of Miss Fennig, the laughter. There are more parts of love than a city has sections, theaters, parks, residence, business, Skid Row.

I move to Frankfurt. To take a higher-paying job teaching illiterate American soldiers. A tedium relieved only by new acquaintance with the bewildered backside of American life: ex-coal miners, fired truck drivers, rattled welterweights, disgraced messengers, sharecroppers, fugitives, the human rubbish conscripted to fill a quota, shoved now into school for the glory of the army. I have the most beautiful single class of my life with them. End of Grade Four. There is a poem in our soldiers' textbook, "The Psalm of Life." *Tell me not in mournful numbers, life is but an empty dream, for it is the soul that slumbers and things are not what they seem.* We go over every word, every line. How they begin to understand, how deeply they know these truths. Sgt. Carmody whose boy is dead in the new Korean war. Gray-haired Private Eady who writes his mother the first letter of his life: "I am in Grad Too, Muther. I work hard every day but Muther, I think it is to lat for me now." Pfc. Coolidge, mouth a fortune of gold teeth, a little black man who joined up after being injured on the job—the Human Missile in Bell and Brother's Circus—and whom I summon to VD Clinic every Monday afternoon. "Dese froolines lak me, perfesser." Carmody, Coolidge, Eady, Dunham, Lake, Barboeuf. The class ends on your breathlessness, your tears, your beautiful silence.

Back home then, to Iowa, to Connecticut, and then here, to the great Gothic hive of instruction and research. Hundreds of classes, hundreds and hundreds of students. Themselves now writing books, teaching classes, building bridges (over rivers, in mouths), editing papers, running bureaus, shops, factories. Or dead in wars, half-alive in madhouses. *"Dear Mr. Wissler. I am in a bad way. No one to write to. There is nothing for me. Help, help, he . . ."* the *"lp"* dropped off the postcard (mailed without return address from Pittsburgh). "Dear Professor Wissler. *Do you remember Joan Marie Rabb who wrote the paper on Julien and Bonaparte in 1964?"* I do remember. For it was a paper so gorgeously phrased and profoundly opaque I called in the dull, potato-faced Miss Rabb to explain it. And with explana-

17

tion—missed connections filled in, metaphors yoked to amazing logic—the potato opened into a terrible beauty. *"I married, Professor. A ruffian, a churl. Children have come. Four, under six. I could not sustain the hurt."* "Miss Rabb, if you can ever put down on paper what you've told me in the office, you will write a work of genius. But for now, you see why I must give you a C." *"You liked the paper, thought it, thought I had promise. What I have done, with great laboriousness, is to transmute it into the enclosed poem. Will you see if the promise is herewith fulfilled? Have I a work which has at least merchandisable power?"* Fifteen penciled pages, barely legible, and when read, wild, opaque, dull. "Dear Mrs. MacIllheny. I look forward to reading your poem when the pressure of the term is over. Meanwhile, I hope you regain your health. With good wishes from your old professor, Charles Wissler."

At times, very few, thank God, there have been students who've rubbed me the wrong way. (How many have I antagonized? Surely many more, but the standards of courtesy are so powerful, only the rudest and angriest breach them.) "I have never, never, never, never, never in my life had a C before. Is it your intention, Mr. Wissler, that I do not go to law school? Do you delight in ruining my *entire academic record?"* Terrifying calm from the plump, parent-treasured, parent-driven face.

"One C does not a bad record make, Ms. Glypher. Admissions Officers know that anyone can have a bad class, an imperceptive instructor."

"Lovely philosophy, sir, but that does not change the C. It does not get me into *law school."*

May I never be cross-examined by Sophia Glypher. "What can I do, Ms. Glypher? Can I change the grading system to accommodate your ambition?" A wicked stare from the not unbeautiful gray eyes. Since you are so clearly

18

intelligent, Ms. Glypher, why is it that you don't see that my standards curve around sweetness, beauty, charm?

"I'll write an extra paper. Retake the exam."

"There are two worlds rotating around each other here, Ms. Glypher. One is the world of papers, exams, grades, degrees, applications, careers. That's a fairly rigid world." (Or unfairly.) "It is as strictly ruled as chess. Break the rules, you break the world. This is the world that's supposed to count. In the other world, there are no grades. In that world you're not a C student. I don't know what you are. Or what I am." Ms. Glypher rumbles here on the verge of a discourtesy which might draw us into open combat. As it is, there is struggle. (Unequal.) "That world's one without end. I see my job more in that world than the one in which I grade you C." Even as I oppose her, wrestle within her magnetic hatred, I believe this. "In that world, we're equal. To some degree partners. Your accomplishment there becomes mine, mine yours. It's the world that counts."

"But not for law school, Mr. Wissler. I don't object to poetry, but I'm talking reality."

"Ms. Glypher, the whole point is that you aren't. You are so attached to the one world that you don't even see it clearly. The Admissions Officers happily do. They will recognize your talent even through what you think of as this stain on your record. If you like, I will put a letter in your dossier explaining my belief in your talent along with the reasons I graded you as I did."

"I don't think I'll trouble you to do that," says Ms. Glypher in her finest moment. One which tempts me to the drawer where the Change of Grade slips are kept.

Before, within, and after classes, the stuff of articles, books, lectures—San Diego, Tuscaloosa, Cambridge—

East and West—, Lawrence, Kansas, Iowa City, Columbia, South Carolina, Columbia, 116th Street, New York, Kyoto, Bologna, Sydney, Buenos Aires, Hull, Nanterre, Leiden. Everywhere wonderful faces, the alert, the genial, the courteous (the bored, the contemptuous, the infuriated; but few). And everywhere, love, with the sexuality displaced (except in the instance which became Wife Number Three). That has been priestly excruciation.

Then pulling toward, docking at and taking off from fifty, I became conscious of the love that has been under all the others. I love individuals, yes, and I stay aware of clothes, bodies, gestures, voices, minds, but it is the class itself I love. The humanscape. The growth of the unique molecule of apprehension and transmission. From the first, tense, scattered day through the interplay, the engagements, the drama of collective discourse to the intimate sadness of the last class. How complicated the history, the anatomy, the poetry of such a body.

Miss Fennig. Mr. Quincy. Mr. Parcannis. Miss Vibsayana. Except for your colors, your noses, your inflections, your wristwatches, I can tell very little about your status. (You are from a warrior caste in Bengal, Miss Vibsayana. You wrote it in a paper. Miss Glennie, you were the brilliant, solitary black girl in the Harrisburg parochial school. You gave me hints of it in office hours.) But I know you inside out; would like to give you all A's. (Won't.) All that part is clear, though Mr. Laroche won't know that the extra paragraph he tacked on his paper lowered his grade from B plus to B; nor Mrs. Linsky that if she'd not spoken so beautifully about Stavrogin, she would not have passed.

December. The last class. There is amorous ether in the room. (Isn't it what Alumni Organizations try to bottle?) Don't we all sense it this last time?

Wissler Remembers

"There's a fine book by the French scholar Marrou on the history of education in antiquity. I recommend it generally, but mention it in this windup class, because it was there I first encountered the idea that there are strikingly different notions of individuality. One sees this also in the first volume of Mann's Joseph series. People hardly know where their ancestors leave off and they begin. That might be straining a bit. Marrou speaks of family identity. Certain Roman families were known for certain sorts of generosity, others for sacrifice. That's certainly still true. Think of American families associated with philanthropy or public service. Even if an individual in the family feels it goes against his grain to go public—as it were"—smiles from Miss Fennig, Mr. Waldemeister—"he is still conscious of the possibility of public life. I don't say that makes it harder or easier for him." Miss Fennig's slim face is alight, her eyes floatingly green under her large spectacles. She runs her hand through her long hair, in, up, out, back. Mr. Quincy's urchin face is stippled—such pain for him—with hormone frenzy. He tries to sit where he can see Miss Fennig. The brilliant, troubled Ms. Shimbel is about to speak. I wait. She shakes her head. How she understands. (Speaking only on demand, resigned from so much, but who knows, perhaps already launched on some intricate enterprise.)

I talk more. I watch. Mr. Parcannis questions. Miss Vibsayana responds, endlessly, softly, the thousand bees of her throat discharging nectar into syllables.

"Forgive me, Miss Vibsayana, what you say is beautiful, but I'm afraid we must finish off."

Wonderful inclination of eyes, head. "Excuse me, Professor."

"Of course. You know how much I enjoy your notions. How much I enjoy all your notions. It has been a splendid class. For me. There is almost no future I think should be denied you. What world wouldn't be better led by you?"

I don't say that. Instead: "I will have office hours next week. If you have questions about your papers, the course, anything at all, please come see me. And come whenever you like next quarter. We haven't gotten as far as I'd hoped, but you've helped get us quite far. Goodbye and good luck to all of you."

We have no tradition of farewell—applause, rapping, waving. Still, the faces compose a fine comprehension of our bond. There is the sweetness of a farewell between those who have done well by each other. (It does not exclude some relief.)

In the hall, Miss Vibsayana approaches. "May I—I don't quite know how to put it, Professor—but I feel privileged that you permitted me to take this course."

"I'm grateful to you for contributing so much to it. Thank you."

Outside, darkness falling into the white lawns. The paths are mottled with clots of ice. The Gothic buildings shine beautifully under the iron filigree lamps. A half-moon hangs off the bell tower.

Bundles of cloth and fur walk home. Hellos, good nights, goodbyes. Talk of exams, of Christmas plans. Snow like hard meringue. Winter looms. And whoops, heart gripped, I'm heading down, hand cushioning, but a jar.

"Oh, Mr. Wissler. Are you hurt?" Miss Fennig. What an embarrassment.

"No, no, not at all." She bends, gives me her bare hand. I hold it and get pulled while I push up. "Thanks so much. My first fall of the year."

"I took two awful ones yesterday," she lies.

22

Wissler Remembers

"I wish I'd been there to pull you up. Thank you again."

"Are you sure you're all right?" Green eyes, unspectacled, tender.

"I'm fine, thank you. I think it's wonderful that our last day should see me being pulled out of the snow by you. I wish you were around whenever I took a tumble."

"I'll try to be. It almost makes me hope you'll fall again."

"I will, Miss Fennig. And I'll look for you. Good night now."

"Good night, Mr. Wissler. Take care."

You too, Miss Fennig. You too, dear Miss Vibsayana. Mr. Parcannis. And LeQuillec, wherever you are. *Gute nacht,* Fräulein Hochhusen. So long, Sergeant Carmody. You too, Ms. Glypher. So long. Take care. Good night, my darlings. All of you. Good night.

Mail

At least it doesn't count as much as it used to: the day saved because of what's in the little steel cave. Age? Resignation? Or is it I care more for what *I* mail?

Still, it's still nice to get nice letters. Out of the unblue blue where people we're not thinking about are thinking about us. Yet not transmuting themselves (and us) into electric pulses in a vast system of immediacy. Just hes and shes, people with individual calligraphy, personal styles.

Even the salutations are special: "Dear Marcus"; "Dear Tuck"; or (one fairly recent style) "Dear Marcus Firetuck." Which is how the letter from Quito started.

The one from Sandra Lukisch began

How I wish I could begin with "Dear Marcus." But I can't. You will always be the one who guided

25

my first scale lines, reshaded my first chloropleth map. So, "Dear Mr. Firetuck."

Sandra is director of the Lukisch Cartographic Service in Melbourne. I haven't seen her for twenty years but remember her better than people who worked in this office last year. In the mid-Fifties, girls wore soft sweaters, cashmere, alpaca, lambswool. (So much memory has to do with clothes, what's inside and what issues from them. Legs, eyes, sweet—unmappable—hills, ridges, thickets; rough trapezoids, astonishing spheres; eye-brightness; smiles: Sandra's was—is?—a dolphin's deep serene; earlobes; nostrils; waists.) I remember Sandra's beautiful maps. They fuse in memory with her delicate roughness. (No standard beauty.)

In my head there are thousands of maps. My dear gone father said he remembered every mouth he ever worked on. To which hyperbole, Fred, my middle son, responded, "Lucky you aren't a proctologist, Grandpa." On the other hand—as it were—who is to gainsay those cavy regions? To any true investigator, every variation of the studied genotype fascinates. Nothing there can be beneath study, if not devotion.

Sandra writes she is getting married. "At forty, Mr. Firetuck. Imagine." Not difficult, Sandra. Hundreds must have thought of spending years beside—and inside—you. (I myself.) "I had to tell you, dear old master. Who first showed me what an isopleth was." (A line which represents a constant value.)

Those who have stayed in our heads, live there as isopleths; though often unrepresentative of anything but themselves. They are their own color, flag, fruit and meat, the country of Their Self. Sandra stands for Sandra. And for the feelings rising as she re-enters the lit part of my head with her two sheets of typescript. Bless you, Sandra. I will send something or other to Melbourne for you and your fortunate air force colonel. (Did he use your maps?)

The letter from Ecuador was something else. Last March, a fellow called me at my hotel there. I'd flown in from the Cartography Congress in Buenos Aires to give my little spiel on Andean mapping in relation to the new high-resolution photographs we'd been getting from a hundred thousand feet. Joachim ("but called Jock") Fopper had seen the notice of my talk in *El Comercio*. (The good newspapers of that splendid little town may not have sufficient news to fill their local pages.) He wondered if the speaker could be

> the same man who'd written *Reliefs*. I did not think 'Marcus Firetuck' could be so common a name in your country.

It is the only time in my life that this has happened. In a foreign country—and not one of the world's most populous or worldly—someone who is not a cartographer, textbook publisher or military man has not only heard of me, but knows me in that tiny—if intense—part of my life of which *Reliefs* is the only—can I say?—monument.

A forty-four-page chapbook printed by a West Virginia press which "split the cost of printing" with me, *Reliefs* received two reviews (that I've seen, for there's no clipping service which hunts down the places in which reviews of such books appear). Yet Joachim—Jock—Fopper of Quito, Ecuador, not only owned a copy of *Reliefs*, had not only read and apparently found it—I can hardly credit and won't repeat his compliments—but he'd located—

"through friends in New York whom I commission to send me little magazines from the Gotham Book Mart"—eleven of the fewer than twenty other poems I've published in publications, only one of which, *Poetry*, in my own home-town, prints more than two thousand copies an issue. Most of these journals bear the names of small animals—*Raccoon, Marmoset, Gnat*—and print fewer than five hundred copies. Yet out of this black hole of literature, Joachim Fopper had fetched a couple of hundred lines of Marcus Firetuck. "Your work meant something to me from the first three lines I read," he'd told me on the phone last March. And, no dispenser of vapor, he cited—I assume from memory—three lines from "Scratches on the Record": "'They do not mean to hurt the music/They were not made by a mind/ And no one will ever try to reproduce them. . . .'"

These lines had "spoken to" Mr. Fopper. Mr., *Herr*, or *Señor* Fopper. There were tiny Germanic tilts in his close-to-perfect English. Yet, as his letter informed me, he'd lived "twenty-odd years" on "this God-forsaken continent." I had asked him on the phone if he were a poet. "No. Unfortunately." He did not say then, nor does he say in his letter what he was (or is). He had just seen the notice in the newspaper; he was astonished, then thrilled at the notion that it might be "the very man" who had given him "such immeasureable pleasure." (Do I detect a stylistic influence of Firetuck in Fopper? The love of internal rhyme, verbal repetition, the mix of stiffness and idiom?) He did not dare to ask me to have a drink, he had hesitated a long time before telephoning, he did not want to be one of those importunate "voice-tremblers" who "intrude" into the lives of those who had "already done so much" for them.

I was travel-and-lecture weary, and also low: Ethel had

Mail

flown back to Chicago from Buenos Aires and the cartographers here assumed that I was being taken care of by "someone else." (Sweet Quiteño modesty.) So, after our seminar, I was deposited at the *Colon Internacional* in a heap of weary loneliness. I suppose I should have asked Fopper to have dinner with me—the hotel food was terrific—but, who knew, intelligent as he seemed, and surely as sympathetic, wasn't it better to let well-enough be enough?

I did tell him how much his call meant. "This isn't an everyday occurrence, Mr. Fopper. I am not exactly Lord Tennyson or T.S. Eliot. You've cheered me up considerably."

I don't think he was set on meeting me. I believe Fopper is one of those true readers whose truest passion is literary. To encounter the actual flesh of authors (or their characters) would be a gross intrusion on their perfectly adjusted mental life. His phone call was, then, very daring. His letter is only slightly-less so. Perhaps if I were a more prolific poet, Fopper would not try to drill for epistolary firetuckery.

The letter—about two thousand words long—is almost entirely literary. It begins by quoting

> one of the three French poets born in Montevideo, Jules Laforgue. The others, as I do not have to tell you, are Jules Supervielle and the astonishing Isidore Ducasse, the self-styled Comte de Lautréamont.

(He did not have to tell me, but I would have gone to my grave—not necessarily less happily—not knowing.)

> I know a small master's career is, as Laforgue writes, 'decked out with rags and praise' (*'Un train pavoisé*

29

d'éstime et de chiffons'), but I could not resist trying to sew in my rag. I hope it did not disturb you.

From this variation of his oral apology for "intruding," he goes on to the most intricate and subtle criticism I have ever had (and I include reviews of my professional—cartographic—publications). There are comparisons of my poems to ones in four languages, including poems by Americans of whom I've never heard.

An amazing performance by a true amateur of poetry. An amateur of Firetuck. An extraordinary letter. An extraordinary pick-me-up. (How I wish it could be sold in the drugstores between Valium and Mepro-probane. *Fopper's Uppers.)*

But who is or what was Joachim—Jock—Fopper? I wonder now, and in Quito, a bit nauseous and dizzy from the height disease they call *soroche,* I wondered then. (Sucking the nausea-fighting barley sugar candy given me by an English salesman, my seatmate from Buenos Aires.) Once I even wondered if Fopper's call were not a distortion of my dizziness. And later, over pickled *camarones* (the local shrimpy shrimp) and some *sopa quiteño* (egg and white cheese in a rich soup), served in the white and silvery dark elegance of a *Colon Internacional* dining room, I pursued the hints of vertigo to conjure up careers for Herr Señor Fopper. One was shaped by decades of reading mystery and spy novels. So: Joachim Fopper, the only one of the two hundred million people living on the enormous continent who knew Marcus Firetuck as a poet, one of the, say, fifteen? ten? human beings who had been enriched, expanded, *pleased* by my poems—the strangest and most beautiful of mental handshakes—this fan of mine was some Nazi-dribble who'd crawled out of Europe via the Odessa

Mail

Network to South America where his brutal talents went underground to emerge only in such perverse passions as admiration for the obscure poems of a North American— and *for repentance*—Jew. Didn't such careful study of the obscure bespeak training, say, on Admiral Canaris's Counter-Intelligence staff? Indeed, might Fopper's "intrusion" be a subtle way of establishing an American contact?

"Tell me about yourself," I will write back to Fopper.

Or should I? Here in Chicago, with the day's rich mail, his four single-spaced typewritten sheets create an island of international lucidity on my desk. Between matt-finished cellulose plastic, calipers, T squares, nomographic charts and cartographic journals, Fopper's letter is a grail of communion. Why should I test it for fool's gold?

For five or six years now, my steadiest correspondent has been another man with whom I've had next-to-no physical contact. In the spring of 1973, I got away from a tumultuous house party my older children were throwing in our house in Door County and lunched myself in a restaurant in Sister's Bay. At the next table was an enormous young fellow whose head, I remember thinking then, could have been put up almost intact alongside the four Presidents carved out of the South Dakota mountain. As I was marveling at this stony, eyeglassed immensity, it turned my way and asked if it could borrow the sweetener in my sugar bowl. That began a monologue which ended with an exchange of addresses, and this, in turn, became an epic correspondence, the most intense and one-sided correspondence of my life (excluding a shorter one with my first fiancée, Mary Joe Weil—pronounced "wheel"—of Durham, North Carolina, back in the early months of 1952). It is certainly the most peculiar.

Vernon Bowersock.

Is he out of his mind?

I think not. Vernon is just out of your mind, at least out of mine. Or was then. By now I'm used to him. Vernon is one of the very few people who very early on is hooked by a life project. His project is self-reflexive. That is, Vernon is concerned with Vernon. Or, at least, with a kind of vernonization of the world. Vernon wishes to make sense of everything he has seen, heard, or can think about. His tools are numerology and epic poetry. Vernon is always thinking "Where will this or that fit into the *Vernoniad*?"

There is a lot of *this and that*. Vernon runs up and down the United States getting a degree in one thing here, a degree in something else there. He marries, he separates, he divorces. He reads, he carries on his napoleonic correspondence, and he supports himself wherever he goes as a computer programmer. (Knowing such work was useful in any city, Vernon took it up in high school.) Vernon is not a careless man. Indeed, a theme of the future *Vernoniad* is that there is nothing accidental; everything belongs in the great scheme called Vernon.

Vernon was born in the only Mississippi county which seceded from the Confederacy (or does one say "stayed loyal to the Union"). His grandfathers have been the county sheriffs. "As close to being dictator as humans can get in this country," says Vernon. So it is out of this singular world of authority and pride that the future epic poet comes.

Future poet. There's the rub. Vernon has only prepared to write his epic. What's written now is introductory matter. Perhaps Vernon, dazzled so by the possibility of the *Vernoniad*, will write nothing but Introductions. But if one includes the letters to his four chief correspondents—

Mail

"my four compass points"—Vernon's prose already con-
stitutes an epic, a kind of Epic of Introduction.

I answer one in ten or twelve of Vernon's letters. (He
doesn't require answers from his Easts and Wests: the
three others are a preacher in Binghamton, Alabama, an
undertaker in Lompoc, California—"picked because it's
the setting for W. C. Fields' *Bank Dick*"—and a "beautiful
seventy-year-old librarian in Lima, Ohio, so I can begin
her letters, *'Ohi-o'*—'hello' in Japanese, I'm told—'Lovely
Lima Lady Libe.'") Why do I answer them at all? Because
through Vernon I see much of the country and encounter a
mentality my small, skeptical intelligence habitually re-
jects. I suppose too that Vernon's numerology is a wild
form of that impulse which made me both cartographer
and "lisper in numbers," a desire to achieve clarity by
reduction.

Vernon, always in "financial holes bigger than canyons," "thrown out by three wives, all of whom I love and
will always love," always working, reading, moving on and
writing about it all, is, I suppose, my own Odysseus, the
moving part of my essential inertness. I have been in fifty
or sixty countries, but almost always in ways which
eliminate their strangeness; Vernon has never left this
country, but every inch of it is different for him.

163 Farrell Ave.
#19
St. Paul, Minn.

Dear Mr. Firetuck,
    It is 6:18, and I have consumed the day's second
thousand calory. I took a four mile walk, jogged two,
did ninety push-ups, forty kneebends. Tomorrow, I

33

go for my weekend at the Sunfare Camp. I go twice a week. Erections are forbidden. Joke: "When do the Japanese have elections?" "Before bleakfast." I am twenty-nine years, three months, four days, six hours and thirty-one minutes old. I was conceived when George Marshall was making his Marshall Plan speech at Harvard University. Or close to it. You were conceived when Babe Ruth was hitting the twenty-seventh or eighth of his record-breaking sixty home runs. Lindbergh was en route to Paris when your—excited?—parents conceived you. *"Le hasard infini des conjunctions."* (Mallarmé, *Igitur*—I know only this quote which is scrawled on the back-flap of Irma Rombauer's *Joy of Cooking* which work I slobber over as I eat my broiled turbot—120 calories, 200 with Tartar Sauce and catsup. How about the infinite romance of consolation to balance the infinite chance of conjunction?)

I owe twenty-one thousand, nine hundred and seventy dollars, eight thousand of them to Rosaleen who will let me pay back the others first. (She is in Spokane, earning good money in a carob and soy-beanerie.)

Your friend,
Vernon Bowersock

Imagine. I was spawned in an heroic time. My loving progenitors were excited by Lindbergh's flight. (Had they come out of a newsreel theater? Did they exist then? Or had they news on the radio? Did they own one in 1927? No. Too new.) Still, the excitement was in them, the market was good. What a grand time to be conceived? Does it account for the essential peace of my unheroism?

Mail

My own son, Frederick Gumbel Firetuck, was, I'm almost certain, conceived the night Ethel and I went out to Midway Airport with other lost-causers of 1957 to greet Adlai Stevenson's plane. Carl Nachman was there, and he was paying lots of genteel attention to Ethel; much as I liked him, my old jealousy was roused, and, that night, her body roused me like a new one. Fred sprang from that passion. Which explains—why not?—his blue eyes, his exceptional strength and height, his sweet reserve. Why not?

> 3126 Walnut Street
> Evansville, Indiana

Dear Mr. Firetuck,

You'll note I've moved again. A bit of trouble in Sunfare. A forty year old blond-headed, brunette-pubed lady from Milwaukee. Someone with such prodigious endowment should not be allowed the good clean health-fare fun of the colony. It was not before bleakfast, *mais* I was elected. Bad show. The saintly Mr. Carmichael was taking his matutinal walk in the sun and nearly tripped over the barrier. He is like Voltaire's Jesus, "an enthusiast of good faith with a weakness for publicity." I was summoned, marked—though within terrible half-seconds my guilty member had resigned its office—and asked to remove it and its base. Life here in the besummered north is not for such as I anyway. I am Floridian—"oh Florida, venereal soil,"—and I don't have the manners of you northerners.

I weigh 179, though I have not eaten today and on the road was down to fifteen hundred greasy calories.

I'm on Page 134 of three books, pocket jobs. I will now advance to page 184 of each. The books: *Back Swing*, a novel; *The Arnheiter Affair; My Days with the Mafia*.

Do you realize what half a century of life means? It eases my terrible approach to the *mezzo del cammin*.

Your friend,
Vernon Bowersock

There is only one other real letter in this day's mail. (I don't discount the documentary value of dental bills, charity appeals, advertising flyers, and treasure packages, expected—subscriptions, say—or unexpected—perhaps forgotten; but they are not the essence of mail.) The letter is from my old pal, Lester Doyle, whose father was my teacher in Ann Arbor. (Working for the State Department in 1942-44, Prof. Doyle mapped the boundaries which became the three—later four—zones of post-war Germany.) Lester, a poly-progenitor, has not otherwise been as productive as his father. Nor has his life been as serene. Almost every Lester-letter contains at least one piece of bad news. Yet so considerate a person is pale, tiny Lester that he manages to find some countervailing sweetness to enclose with the month's misfortune. He has so large a family—five boys, three girls—that there is always a supply of each on which to draw.

Lester teaches musicology at a remote branch of the University of Arkansas. As the only faculty member who has published an article, he has become a figure of both awe and exoticism. "I am their Paris and their Greece," he wrote me once. "But they are so remote. And so, it appears, am I." I've wondered if Lester's incessant progeniture is an attempt—like his letters—to people solitude.

36

Mail

Today he writes that William, his second son, has had a leg amputated. "Soft-tissue sarcoma, I'm afraid, and the prognosis is not good." I hardly know William Doyle, remember only a frail, shy, small-chinned young man, a young edition of the professorial grandfather for whom he was named. William, like all Doyles, is very intelligent. He got scholarships to Milton and Williams where he was a brilliant student of something like Provençal. A pro football freak, he knows the lifetime won-and-lost records of every professional team. He must be about twenty-two and works for the Atlanta Braves baseball team (doing something with season subscriptions). "Eileen has gone to stay with him." Eileen is his oldest sister.

I was there for several days after the operation. William was very brave. I cannot bear the thought that we might lose him. Yet just that, we have been told, is what will soon happen.

There is other Doyle news, busy news, grandchildren conceived and jobs changed; then there is a paragraph about his research.

I am trying to complete an article on Delphine Potocka, the randy countess who had an affair with Chopin. Chopinologists are most exercised about the subject. A lady in Warsaw discovered a cache of letters in 1945. Or did she? You can imagine what life in Warsaw was like then. Is it unreasonable to see a starving lady scholar filling her belly with the invention of her head? I don't think poor Mme. Czernicka capable of forging them. For instance, there's a line from "Chopin" about wanting to set "something

37

precious in D flat." That is a pun on the most intimate part of a woman's anatomy. Human beings surprise, but I would be very surprised to see Mme. Czernicka making this up.

Little William Doyle prepares to leave the world, and his loving father Lester works to fill the gap with a perhaps-affair of the melancholy genius. Giving Chopin this bit of post-mortuary life, does Lester somehow provide for his son?

The word "mail"—I've looked it up—derives from the Old High German *malha,* a wallet. Its homonym, the woven metal rings used for armor, derives from Old French *maille,* link, and the Latin *macula,* stain.

I like to think of the lexic-twins in Siamese unification: so in these small sacks, these envelopes, we inscribe our little *maculae,* the spots and stains of our individuality. Some we show to one correspondent, some to another. And the result is a mesh of strands from all parts of the world and of our lives. Against the day's brute fact, the fatigues and routinage of *now,* this mesh armors us.

Sandra Lukisch, Joachim (Jock) Fopper, Vernon Bowersock and Lester Doyle, and even you, Fréderick Chopin (or your letter-writer, Mme. Czernicka), though none of you has met or will meet except in my head, on my desk, you are citizens of the country of correspondence, the soul of commerce across time and space; you are society itself.

Beloved correspondents, blessed institution, may the terrible convenience of speedier linkage never triumph completely over your clumsy, difficult frailty. "Very sincerely yours, Marcus Firetuck."

The Ideal Address

1

Everybody close to Winnie's center was in motion.

Fred, no kid anymore, was doing what he'd been doing for three years, crisscrossing the country, following—he told her in collect calls from Phoenix or Fargo—"leads." That is, friends—often met the week before—who had houses to build, acres to plant, jobs to offer, places to crash. Then it was arrival, and weeks, or days, twice, *hours* later, departure. For every amical ointment, a fly. "Ma, the guy lies around all day getting wasted. Good drugs is all there is here. It's one bad scene." Failure of mission reported to Chicago, Fred would be on the road again, thumb cocked, life's accumulation in his rucksack, the Ideal Address summoning him from a few miles, a few states away. "I'm down to twelve bucks. But I don't want anything, Ma. This low, I'll have to stick somewhere."

Twenty-four.

At twenty-four, Winnie had two children, two degrees and supported four people selling southside Chicago lots. Supportee Number Four was the Greater Frederick, rounding the last turn of his eight-year doctorate. The Great One had passed to his namesake blond charm, the gift of living off women, and—might as well face it—a deep tract of sheer dumbness, a power of self-delusion from which contempt or dislike washed easily. (The Fredericks couldn't be snubbed.) "Stick anywhere, Freddy. Build up a stake before you move on. You have to eat lots of dirt before flowers bloom in your face. The planet offers no perfect situations."

"I stuck New York, Ma."

Six months in the *Newsweek* morgue, long enough—to the day—to qualify for battered New York's Unemployment Compensation. Eighty dollars a week, which, with his girl's salary, gave him the life of not-Riley, but Oblomov.

An Oblomov who discovered the Off-Track Betting parlors. And won. Spectacularly. Twenty-three thousand dollars, fourteen on one daily double. "You know the way accountants look at a sheet of figures and see the shape of corporations. Ma, I look at those dope sheets and I *see* the race."

Close to six-and-a-half feet, a hundred and ninety pounds, the green eyes glistening with this dummheit. Yet, the pudding had proved out: twenty-three thousand dollars. "Freddy, now it's time to take the journalism course. Go up to Columbia."

"It's not time for that, Ma."

"Look, Fred, it never hurts for anyone to talk to a counselor. Why not spend a few bucks and get your head

40

cleared? Find out what you'd be best doing, why you're not doing it."

"I'm doing it."

She sensed he was going to stick the money in a hole, not report it to the IRS. "Fred, the tax men are everywhere. They get reports from the OTB every day. Don't conceal anything. Every dollar lights up those computers in Virginia. Don't wiggle."

Was she trying to subdue the divinity of idleness, she who'd burnt offerings to its opposite number since she was nineteen? All those mortgages and leases smoking in the golden nostrils.

Fred went to Aqueduct, he'd never seen the track itself before; the actuality needled his balloon. "All these bums in funny hats coming up to *me* for tips. I'm standing around in my Kenyon sweatshirt, and they're asking *me*." It was another sliver of his pride that no one in New York dressed as badly as he did. In New York! It was like the man in Chekhov who was identified as "Lubov, the one who lost his galoshes at the Balanoffs'."

A month later, in a manner hidden from—and hardly credible to—her, Freddy was down to seven thousand dollars, six of which he put into a mutual fund. "I've been studying the Street, Ma." (He watched *Wall Street Week* on the educational channel.) "What baffles people?"

With the seventh thousand, he "cleared the post," left girl, apartment (the lease had two months to go), and a phone bill, which she, his permanent address, paid. And headed—*tailed* was a better verb for Fred—west. "I might have a day with you in Chicago, Ma. But Jack's in a hurry. He's got a pad in Sonoma County, he says there are millions of jobs in the wineries. And it's more beautiful than the south of France."

He did stop for a day, but she was just moving in with Tom. Fred never liked her boyfriends, and he missed the old apartment, so he and his two pals (the third was picked up in Ohio, a Marx-bearded dreamer who ate one of Tom's plants) stayed only a night. "There's no place in Chicago for me anymore, Ma."

"It's a big city, Fred. You can go down to Hyde Park with Dad."

"Dad doesn't see where I'm at."

Fourteen inches shorter, plain and dumpy as a muffin next to this green-eyed giant, Winnie couldn't bring herself to ask where he was. He was so hugely *there*. Besides, she had all she could handle now with Tommy.

2

The reason she'd moved in with him after twelve years in her own place was his desperation. A month ago, he'd been "dumped" by his analyst, and had imploded, collapsed. He couldn't get out of bed. The black pearl eyes which sat out on his gold cheeks dropped tears down them. "Why did he do it to me, Winnie? What did I do wrong? Was it the writing? He knew I was writing the book."

Tom was finishing a doctorate, writing on the nature of evidence in psychoanalysis. One section recorded his own reactions to fifteen analytic sessions and was to be followed by Dr. Culp's notes on the same sessions. It would be a unique document, real material for students of the profession. But Culp slammed the door. The impassive, lunar face which had dominated Tommy's dreams for two years, burned with rage. While Tom was on the couch, Culp called Dr. Fried and told him he thought it was time to turn Mr. Hiyashi over to him. Tom fainted, was revived, staggered up the hall and found two doctors and three cops—"with guns, Win"—would he sign himself in or did he prefer to be committed by Culp? "You were signaling you wanted to be hospitalized," Culp said when he finally agreed to talk to Tom.

Winifred got Tom out. She went to Professor Kluger-man, he found someone to sign for Tom, then gave her the word on Culp: Chicago was littered with his wrecks, he'd been a promising young man, but his own problems had ruined him; he was ok when the transference was rosy; when it got rough, he abandoned ship, hospitalized the patients and told them he couldn't work with patients who'd been hospitalized.

Psychoanalysis is the best-protected fortress in the world; its stones are invisible; even with a Klugerman on one's side, a malpractice suit was next to impossible.

Anyway, Tom was too low to think of litigation. For two years, all the feeling in the world was held by the four walls of Culp's office. Now he'd never see him again. "Analysis may not have the power to cure, it sure has the power to hurt." Tears dropping on the gold cheek flesh. "I can't think of anything else, Win." Even now, two months after Winnie had moved in, five weeks after he'd started with Dr. Fried, Tom's head was a Culp museum. He parked near Culp's house, gawked at his wife and children, took pictures of the garden, the cars. "Win, yesterday I wanted to steal his garbage. A big sack of garbage, and I wanted it."

"Oh, Tommy."

"Maybe because I was his garbage. And I gave him all mine. I gave him all the crap in my head, and he told me to get out. He's supposed to take it. An analyst is an

43

incinerator. No, a recycling plant. But he cycled me out. How would you feel, Win?"

"I know, Tommy, I know," stroking him, the handsome little black-top head, the beautiful little shoulders.

She knew a little anyway, she'd been dumped as well, and not by a passing stranger. The Greater Frederick had finished his dissertation, acknowledged "its essential ingredient, my wife," and four years later, just starting to make enough money so she could stop making it and concentrate on her poetry, he discovered that "everything on this earth has a term," they "had had the best of marriage, the worst was coming," it was "time to think of 'fresh fields and pastures new,' old Win."

Of course he'd been plowing the new pasture for a year. Stroking Tom, Winnie remembered her own obsession with Rosanne, looking her up, what a shock, a scrawny kid, rearless, breastless, with a nose that hooked wickedly toward her teeth. A classic Frederickan delusion. (Line up, Rosanne.)

Eight years, they lived five blocks apart. So the move to Tommy's had the relief of that separation as well. And maybe some of the relief of Freddy's moving; moving for its own sake, though she believed what she'd quoted at him from Donne, "For there is motion also in corruption."

"Corrupt, Ma?"

"No, Freddy, it's just that motion isn't necessarily healthy."

"You could sell it to Weight Watchers. I always lose five or six pounds a trip. You should try it for that alone, Ma."

She didn't need that. Her weight was what she had. "Lose enough, you can fit in an envelope, mail yourself to yourself. You'd never catch up. Ride round the earth for the price of a stamp. Need the dime?"

The Ideal Address

"You're some punkins, Ma." Harshness slid from him. (He always gained his five pounds back.)

The move did occupy her, and it blurred some of Tom's first shock and the brevity of Freddy's stay; and then Nora's hysterectomy, which came ten days after Freddy left.

She had "never been close" to Nora was what she told friends, what she thought, but of course that was too easy. Nora had been in her belly and at her breast, she'd loved her wildly, as she'd loved Freddy. But when Frederick took off, Nora, though she stayed with her mother, took off too. Eight years old, and Winifred would see the green eyes flashing chill at her, the unvoiced indictment: "You let what counted get away, you weren't good enough to hold it. Are you what I have to be? Is that what a girl is? Someone left?"

But over the phone, Nora wept, she was never going to have her own child, and Winnie took off for Denver and held Nora's blonde head on her breasts, she mustn't worry, she and Francis could adopt ten babies, it was the right thing to do in this 1970s world, the hysterectomy was a sign her system would have trouble with babies, she would have all the joy—and almost all the difficulties—of children, the genetic part was insignificant.

She stayed two weeks, doing chores, keeping cheer, even had the first good talks of her life with Nora, it looked as if at last they would be friends. But toward the end, the new grievance must have revived the old, she looked up to the green eyes flaming at her. "You don't know your own nature, Momma."

"Maybe I'd run away from myself if I did."

"No. If you knew where you were, what you are, things wouldn't happen *to* you all the time. You'd happen to

45

them." Nora, white as a bathtub, with only her green eyes
for color.

"I'm not much on all this knowing thyself. That's what
our Fredericks are after, or say they are. 'Where's that
Great Phone Book in the Sky with my number in it?'
What's the point, Nora? Look at Tom." Nora never
wanted to look at Tom. "Ten years on the S.S. Couch, and
what's his America? Shipwreck. 'I'm too busy for that,' as
Pat Nixon told Gloria Steinem. Right on. And if you want
better authority for burying the self, go to Jesus. Or
Buddha. Or Jane Austen. George Eliot. Did they squat
around asking who they were?" But Nora would write no
book, adopt no child. "I'm just dodging, Nora. You're
right."

It was time to go. Francis took her to the airport. "I can
be back in hours if you need me, Francis."

"You're a brick, Win." Endless, vague, unbricklike
Francis.

3

Solid, maybe dumpy Winnie, yes, a bit of a brick, but,
on her own, had put two children through Lab School and
college, had moved more southside noncommercial real
estate than anyone in the city, could have had her own
firm, been a rich woman, if she hadn't hated being a boss
(firing people, fighting the IRS). She was a brick, and then
some, a lot of bricks, and some windows, doors, and not a
bad interior, ask Tom, ask a few discriminating human
beings.

The Ideal Address

But in need of tuck pointing, chimney work.

Mornings, waking up next to Tom (unless he was out casing Culp's garbage), her head was full of nutty projects: she'd form an Effluvium Corporation, market the leavings of the great (Picasso's shaved hairs, Elizabeth Taylor's sweat, a bottled ounce for eighty bucks); or she'd discover Jesus's *Autobiography. The Word first? No. Words come from throats. I was born in almost the usual way. In a backwater town.*

Breakfast up here was nice. Tom's place was across the street from Wrigley Field, and in the morning, or on days there was no ballgame, the neighborhood felt as if it had fallen out of the present tense. The streets zoomed up to the great oval and died; the silence was spectral. There were lots of Koreans and Japanese around—they'd come from California after World War II—the small business streets had a special feel, old ladies bowing to each other, Shinto shrines and rock gardens behind standard Chicago threeflats, the *kanji* script on the hardware and grocery stores suggesting intense messages from the clouds.

Ballgame days, the morning silence thickened into noise, vendors wheeled their carts, the pennant men and car-parkers warmed their throats for the crowd as it poured in under the windows.

What was that crazy mass they celebrated in the oval? (The little white grail pounded and pitched.)

She sat in Tommy's "greenhouse" room, doing her accounts, reading poetry, or just dreaming of something happening, something working, Freddy settling in, Nora taking care of a baby (knowing what feelings you couldn't allow yourself in the depth of that dependence), Tom shifting the hump of trouble from Culp to Fried.

A stillness in others so that her own motion would count.

47

She didn't want ease, she was even tired of not being tired, of trouble washing too easily out of her system. (Inside, she was brick.)

She wasn't ready to hit the road. (What road was there?) Down the street was far enough.

> . . . Green Chill upon the Heat
> So ominous did pass
> We barred the Windows and the Doors
> As from an Emerald Ghost—

That childless lady in white who never left her room.

> The Doom's Electric Moccasin . . .
> The Blonde Assassin passes on . . .
> imperceptibly . . . lapsed away

For Emily D., the motion of the world was sinister.

But poems didn't do the trick today. They handled too much, stood for too much. (As the accounts stood for too little: Illinois Bell Tel., Consolidated Ed.)

The Oval burst. Home run.

She'd left home, but not arrived. Hidden in Tom's green world, little insectless, birdless, snakeless jungle, so much less jungle than his mind.

Or hers.

Born? In the usual way. Not knowing. Daughter, mother, but alone. Without ideal address.

Packages

As I was staying in Aliber's place across from Campbell's, my sister asked me to pick up the package. "I guess it's the acknowledgment cards." Our mother had died five days before.

Campbell's is a wonderful funeral factory. It does it all for you, gets the notice into the *Times,* sends for the death certificates (needed by banks, lawyers, accountants), orders the printed acknowledgments of condolence, and of course works out the funeral; or, as in Mother's case, the cremation and memorial service.

We'd held the service there in the large upstairs salon. Lots of flowers and few mourners: Mother's friends—who were in New York and ambulatory (eight octogenarian widows)—cousins, many of whom we hadn't seen in decades, two of my children, Doris's, and my father with Tina and Leona, the two Trinidad ladies who kept him up

49

to snuff. A black-gowned organist—the closest thing to a religious figure in attendance—played some of Dad's favorites, "Who," "Some Enchanted Evening" and "Smoke Gets in Your Eyes" (this one a bit much in view of Mother's chosen mode of disintegration).

The package was wrapped in rough brown paper tied with a strand of hemp which broke when I hoisted it. "Don't worry," I said to the shocked Mr. Hoffman. "I'm just across the street." I held it with one hand and shook his with the other. Outside, limousines and chauffeurs idled—it was a slow death day in New York.

Thursday. Garbage-collection on East 81st. A massif of sacks and cartons ranged the stony fronts of town and apartment houses. No one but me on the street. Across Fifth Avenue, the Museum fountains poured boredom into the July heat. I left the package in a half-empty carton, walked to Aliber's door, then returned and covered it with yesterday's *Times*. Back to the house, key in the door, then back again to the package, which I unwrapped. It was a silvery can, the size of a half-gallon of paint; labeled. Curious about the contents, I tried to open it. No lid. Nor was it worth the trouble of fetching a hammer and wedge from Aliber's. I stripped off the label, rewrapped the can, and covered it with the newspaper. On top of that, I put a plasticine sack of rinds and fishbones.

Aliber's apartment is dark, leathery, high-ceilinged, somberly turbulent. Its walls are books. Books litter tables, chairs, sills, floors. An investment counselor, Aliber is really a reader. His claim is that all intelligence has a monetary translation. A cover for sheer desire to know everything. (He does better than most. Of the hundreds of Aliber books I've looked at, ninety per cent bear his green-inked comments.)

50

Packages

There are hours to kill before Doris picks me up. I activate air conditioners and sound system and pick out some correct music. A cello suite of Poppa Bach. Naked on the leather couch, I listen until it overflows my capacity. You need weeks for such a piece. It should take as long to listen to as it did to compose. Or is the idea to reduce vastness into something portable?

A package.

I think I thought that then, though the notion may have come after I'd found *The Mind of Matter* in the wall behind my head. I read a chapter devoted to Planck's "famous lecture to the Berlin Academy in May of 1899," in which he described "that extraordinary quantity" which "for all times and cultures" made possible "the derivation of units for mass, length, time and temperature." Planck's constant. Not then called h. Only 6.625×10^{-27} erg seconds, or, by our author, "that stubby transmitter of universal radiance . . . Nature's own package." Little as I understood of this package, I felt some connection between it and Bach's and the one which held what was left of what had once held me.

Six weeks earlier, back in Chicago, I'd written a letter in my head. *Dearest Mother. Last Saturday, I unbuttoned your dress and slipped it off your shoulders. Doris undid your bra, and for the first time in decades, I saw your sad breasts. We put the gauzy, small-flowered nightgown over your head and pulled it down the bony tunnel of your back, your seamed belly.*

Before we taxied to Mount Sinai, Leona fixed your hair; tucked, curled, waved and crimped it. (If her eight months of beauty school produce nothing else, they've been worth it.) It was your last home vanity. When we left you, sunk in the narrow bed, the piled hair survived. Your stake in the great world.

I finished lunch with my spring wheat man in the Wrigley Restaurant and walked alone by the Chicago River. Immense brightness, the Sun-Times Building a cube of flame. All around, the steel-and-glass dumbness of this beautiful, cruel town. *I noticed, then noticed I noticed, the bodies of women, white and black. Thank you, Mother, for my pleasure in such sights.*

A girl in leotards the color of papaya meat jumped around a stage in front of the big nothing of Picasso's metal gift—bloodless heart, brainless head. Huffing, she explained arabesque and second position to the soft crowd of municipal workers, shoppers, tourists. It's splendid being part of a crowd like this, letting bored respect for art muzzle the interest in the dancer's body. Bless such civic gifts.

There have been times I've wanted your death, Mother. At least, did not much care.

It was money. That noise. Curse me for it.

I've walked through slums, *bustees, barriadas, callampas, favelas, suburbios* (the very names a misery). *In a Calcutta dump, I saw a darker you,* forty years younger, everything in her life within her reach: pot, shawl, kid. *What should a man do with money?* Getty, the billionaire, claimed he wasn't rich, didn't have a spare—an *uninvested*—nickel. I'm rich. So what am I doing in these glassy dollared Alps—reflections annihilating reflections—the money canyons of your town and mine?

Unearned dough. *It came to you without effort; it filled your head. (Should noise fill heads like yours? Or mine?)*

Last week you said you wanted "to go" and you kissed me with the strength of goodbye. (Goodbye is what's left.) *Soon you'll be nothing but your purses, your spoons, your china, your sheets, your doilies. Your money. You'll be an absence in Doris; in me, a shard in Dad's head.*

After Mother's death—which he does not acknowledge: she is *out for lunch*—his head is in more of a whirl than ever. He shuts himself in closets, undresses at three P.M., goes, pajamaed, into the street (brought back by the doormen). One night, he appears naked at Tina's bedside. He says he wishes to do things with her. Disused parts hang from his groin like rotten fruit. Tina gets a blanket around him, persuades him back to his own bed. "I was *so* scared, Miss Doris. Doctor is a strong mon. Yesterday, he move the fuhniture round and round the living room."

Deprived of cigarettes—he sets clothes and furniture afire—and of the *Times*—there's a pressman's strike—his hours are spent walking from room to room, staring at Third Avenue, winding his wristwatch.

As the small shocks of his small world dislodge more and more of his brain, his speech shrivels to the poetry of the very young and old.

"How are you today, Daddy?"

"Rainy."

"What time do you make it?"

"Too late."

He lives by a few lines of verse which embody a creed and an old passion for eloquence. "For a' that and a' that, A man's a man for a' that." (We recite the Burns poem at his grave.) "Oh, lady bright, can it be right/This window open to the night?"

Decades of control slough off the frail body. He sits tensely in the living room. "What you doin', Doctor?"

"Waiting."

53

"May I ask what you waitin' *for?*"

"A girl is coming."

"What gull you talkin' of?"

"None of yours. Give her fifty dollars. A hundred dollars."

Tina has a grand laugh. (And laughs are scarce here.) He is furious. "Out."

He waits an hour, then locks himself in the bathroom.

"You okay, Doctor?"

"Am I supposed to be?"

Doris calls Dr. Rice, who is not surprised. "It's the ones who've done the least who do the most now. I've known them to masturbate in front of people."

"Maybe we should get him a girl."

"I don't think that would do any good. And *he* certainly couldn't."

"What can be done?"

"An extra tranquilizer before bed."

Not a few times we would have liked to tranquilize him permanently. But senility is too part of life, one of the few remaining middle-class encounters with the Insoluble.

One afternoon, before I went back to Chicago, he came in while I was going over estate papers. He was in white pajamas. (The day's familiar divisions were no longer his.) "I have to talk with you, Son."

"What is it, Dad?"

He took a scrap of paper from his old billfold and gave it to me. "I want to go here."

"You are here. This is your address."

"No, dear. I want to go *home.*"

"This is your home. No one else's."

"I don't think so."

Packages

And he was right. Home is where his wife lived. Or his mother—who died during the Spanish-American War.

The next day, his need to go home was so strong, we took a taxi four blocks to Doris's house. How happy he was. Doris was a segment of that female benevolence which had watched over him from birth, mother-stepmother-sisters-wife-daughter. They were a continuity of watchfulness. How he kissed Doris, and talked, until, noticing unfamiliar furniture, a different view, he grew weary. We taxied home, and now it was home, the place where his wife would be coming after lunch.

In Chicago, I got the day's bulletins by phone. "He peed in the dresser."

"Jesus."

"I think he confused drawer and door. They both open. I mean it wasn't totally irrational."

"Bless you, Doris."

He became incontinent. "I never thought I'd live to clean up my own father. I couldn't let the girls do it."

"How long can it go on?"

"Dr. Rice says he's strong as an ox. There's nothing organically wrong."

"Poor fellow."

"He misses you."

"How do you know?"

"He lights up when I say you're coming. Can't you come?"

"I'll try."

But didn't. At Christmas, I sent him a check for a billion dollars. "To the World's Best Father."

"Did he like it?"

"I don't think so. He tore it up."

55

"How dumb of me."

"He's still a human being, you know."

"I hadn't forgotten." *Despite those reports of yours,* I didn't say. *Which convert him into a pile of disasters.* "I should have come. He knew I should be there. And knew I knew it." Unable to say it directly, he tore up the check.

His last paternal correction.

At the end of the beautiful novella which Proust plants like an ice-age fragment in his novel, Swann thinks how terrible it is that the greatest love of his life has been for a woman who was not his type. (This thought—like the piano music of Ravel—detonates the world's pathos for me; though consciousness makes it as beautiful as the music.) My mother was not my type.

A month after Dad's death, I dreamed that she and I were having another of the small disputes which disfigured thousands of our hours. "I can't bear your nagging," I said. As always, my anger silenced hers. She said she'd tell my father to speak to me. But when he came in, he was the old man who died, and, instead of his slipper, I saw only the sad face of his last days.

Then my dream mother said, "I hope you'll be coming back to New York next summer."

"This one hasn't been very pleasant."

"I haven't had a good one either."

I knew this meant the ulcerous mouth, the colds, the drowsiness which disguised and expressed her cancer.

I was about to tell her that I would be back, when this part of the dream became a poem. (My dreams often conclude in poems and interpretations.) On a screen of air, I saw lines from George Herbert's "The Collar." "Forsake thy cage," they read,

Packages

> Thy rope of sands,
> Which petty thoughts have made, and made to thee
> Good cable, to enforce and draw,
> And be thy law . . .

My dream-interpreter here let me know that my cable had turned to sand because my parents were dead. I was free.

I've been a father so long, I didn't know how much I was still a son; how onerous it was to be a son. Now my "lines and life were free." "But," the poem continued on the screen of inner air,

> as I raved and grew more fierce and wild
> At every word,
> Methought I heard one calling, *Child!*
> And I replied, *My Lord.*

My response was not "My Lord" but *My Duty.* The Duty which had raised and formed me.

Only at the beginning of my life and the end of hers did I love my mother wholly. When her life was over—like a simple-minded book—I pitied its waste.

There was much intelligence and much energy in her. Yet what was her life but an advertisement for idleness. And how could such a woman have failed to be a nagger, a boss, the idle driver of others, an anal neurotic for whom cleanliness was not a simple, commonsensical virtue but a compulsion nourished by her deepest need? *Wash your hands. Pick up your clothes. The room is filthy. Eat up. Mary wants to go out.* (The sympathy for Mary veiled the need to have the dining room inert, restored to pre-organic purity. What counted was setting, stage, the scene before and after

57

action. What drastic insecurity underlay this drive towards inertness?)

Too simple.

Mother loved learning, going, seeing. She loved shows, travel, games. She loved *doing good*.

Nor is this enough. She was the reliable, amiable center of a large group of women like herself, the one who remembered occasions and relationships, the one who knew *the right thing to do*.

Her telephone rang from eight A.M. on. Lunches, games, lectures, plays, visits. Lunch was a crucial, a beautiful event. One went *out*. (But where? Longchamps—before its fall—Schrafft's, but which one? *Or shall we try a new place?* What excitement.) Whose game was it? Beasie's? Marion B's? Justine's? Bridge, canasta, gin, mah-jongg (the small clicks of the tiles, "One dot"; "Two crack").

A smallish woman, five-four, brown-haired. (Gray for the last twenty years, but I always *saw* her brown-haired.) Not abundant, but crowded with soft, expressive waves. (Expressive of expense; of free time.) Clear brown eyes, scimitar nose, narrow lips; a sharp face, once soft, fine-cheeked, pretty.

She died well. "What choice do I have?"

Not bad; for anyone, let alone a monument to redundance. (Bear two children, *cared for by others*, oversee an apartment, *cleaned by others*, shop for food, *cooked by others*.) She died bravely, modestly, with decorum. The decorum of practicality. (Her other tutelary deity.) She made up her mind to be as little trouble to those she loved as possible. (Cleanliness reborn as virtue.) She set her face to the wall, stopped taking medicine (without offending the nurses she loved so in the last weeks), and sank quietly into nonexistence. The last hours, teeth out, face caved in, the wrestler

Packages

Death twisting the jaw off her face, she managed a smile (a human movement) when I said we were there, we loved her. She lay, tiny, at the bottom of tremendous loneliness.

Doris and I wait for a taxi at the corner of 81st and Madison. Seven o'clock, the tail end of the day. Traffic flows north. Buses crap plumes of filth into the lovely street (where—I think for some reason—Washington's troops were chased by British redcoats two hundred years ago). A growl of horns to our left. A Rolls-Royce honks at a Department of Sanitation truck in front of Aliber's house. The garbage men are throwing sacks and cartons into great blades whirling in the truck's backside. A powerful little fellow throws in the carton with my package.
"What's the matter?"
"Nothing."
"You look funny."
"Tell you later."
Goodbye, darling.
And: Why not?
You were a child of the city, born here, your mother born here. If I could have pried it open, I would have spread you in Central Park. But this way is better than a slot in that Westchester mausoleum. Foolish, garish anteroom to no house. Egyptian stupidity.
And it was the *practical* thing to do.
Wasn't it, Mother?

Troubles

1

Trouble, Hanna knew, seldom came labeled. And her trouble was not simple sexual confusion. Everyone she knew slid up and down the sexual shaft, getting off first at this floor, then at that one. She herself was one of the straightest of straight arrows. (If there were sexual continents to explore, she was no sexual Alexander.)

The confusion was deeper. Certainly deeper than what diverted her or with whom she slept. Troubles were deep structures. Or structural defects. Deep, confusing, hard to assign. Cagey. Uncageably cagey.

She thought keeping a diary would help. It had helped Kafka (a pillar of her marooned dissertation, *The Dissolving Self in Braque and Broch, Kafka and Kandinsky*). Instead of burrowing into it, she bought a Woolworth notebook and began burrowing into herself, her life with Jay. It went slowly.

Kafka observed himself dissolve, described the dissolution, and put another version of himself together. That was caginess. Her first entry in the speckled, Rorschach-y book dealt with him:

Kafka's lodestone was his father. Is mine Jay? Or myself with Jay? I only know I'm bottled up. But is he the bottle or the bottler?

Or was it the rodent life they led on the periphery of lofty mentality?

They lived like anchorites on the last fifteen hundred dollars of their Peace Corps savings and half-time jobs (Hanna in the law library, Jay tutoring Javanese and Arabic). They ate like health-freaked Saint Anthonys: raw carrots, cottage cheese, cabbage, Bran Buds, fruit, dried milk, beans, soy-substitute "meatoids" (a Jayism) frozen into "tomatoid gunk." "'Poor, forked creatures,' yes," said Jay, "but not poor, forked, *constipated* ones."

They had spent two years among people who owned next to nothing; yet here, in their little white apartment over the Midway, Hanna felt an extraordinary barrenness. If only she had a few plants, something alive to care for.

Hanna was mad for flowers. Nights she got to sleep walking her memory through the forest near Sadjapaht: mangrove, sesamum, cinnamon, palm, banana trees with their edible hives, the casuarinas with whip branches, their sides bunged with vermilion fungi ("jungle whores," Jay called them).

He was no plant lover. "Not in Chicago. Not here." (Their dumbbell-shaped slot tipped over the asphalt-split greens of the Midway.) "A goldfish would crack our little ecosystem. We can't import the jungle." Waving at their

62

walls—puffed and wattled as old Caucasian skin: "We fight the dust for breath."

"Plants would freshen the place."

"Nights?" (When he worked at home, moated by monographs on social stratification, village bureaucracy, shamanism, and apple cores, note cards, dictionaries, the green vase from which he drank decaffeinated coffee. The sacred circle of his absorption.)

He's not cruel. He just hates what he has to do so much, he armors himself against anything that would tempt him from it. As far as he can love anyone, he loves me. He needs insulation. I'm insulation. He's so fragile inside he doesn't want to know about it. He doesn't want to think about himself. This turns out to be more selfish than selfishness. The egocentricity of damaged egos.

For her birthday—the funereal twenty-fifth—he brought home an African violet. He'd scooped and sieved dirt from the Midway—"In Chicago, dirt has to be cleaned"—and planted it in a washed-out jar of Skippy.

"When we get the doctorates, we'll settle in a garden. You can start a vegetable state. Every plant in creation can have its own municipality. You'll be Mother Shrub."

"Oh, sweetheart." Looking at the little purple blossoms.

Which soon curled off. But, eyes to the leaves' small fur, Hanna conjured up Java, the silver alang grass outside the kampong, the ferns, pitcher plants, orchids. Pods, spikes and glumes burst, and fragrance poured over the valley. Transfixed by fatigue, loneliness, heat squatting on every bone, she took in the aromatic ecstasy like some great work of mentality.

Twenty miles away lived the polite, handsome boy she'd met during orientation period in Jakarta. One afternoon, she hitched a samlor ride and was pointed out to him in the paddies (shaded by the nipple-tipped straw hat which, from the road, made him look like an ambulatory mushroom). "Hey, there. Jay. It's Hanna. From Sadjapaht."

How could I tell? I'd have fallen for Dracula if he'd spoken English. Life was so nutty. All that Java courtesy that made you feel transparent. They looked through you. Not even Pua or Madame Charwa talked to me those first weeks.

She and Jay met once a week, hitching samlor or bullock-cart rides until they bought bicycles. The meetings were the week's beacon. On their first three-day leave, they bicycled to Boroboudur and, in a hotel near that old monument to release from world and flesh, they worked out their own release.

Oddly, it was Madame Charwa who first sensed their division. Jay had bicycled over to Sadjapaht the day Pua, the old coffee stallman—her first Javanese friend—died. Everyone in the kampong went to Pua's house. Jay told her to make a bowl of rice and go too, it was their chance to see a funeral *slametan*. She sat with Madame Charwa, Jay with the men. Priests recited Arabic prayers, Pua's black body was undressed, washed, and stuffed with cotton pads. Hanna cried. The Javanese tried to ignore this impropriety. Jay looked icebergs at her, she managed to stop; but confusion had crept into the ceremony, the *santri* hurried the prayers and carried Pua off, Jay after them. Elegant Madame Charwa, more worldly than the others— she was the local representative of the yam-and-pepper cooperative in Surabaya—walked Hanna back to the hut. "One acts as one is trained. Your friend was severe with you. The two of you are not alike. Despite your mutual affection. He is less *djava*." (Less *Javanese*, which meant *less human*.) A peculiar criticism to which Hanna was too far gone in love to attend. Her fear was that she had offended

64

Jay; he would see how badly she acted, how silly she was, and would stop seeing her.

But Jay returned full of what he'd sought. The Javanese temperament suited his own. *Iklas*, the disciplined unfeeling which the funeral *slametan* was supposed to induce, had less assertive snobbery than British "indomitability," less military callousness than Spartan-Roman stoicism. It was an attitude that would do for much of life. *Another mask for his fragility,* she would write in her diary account of these memories.

In their second Indonesian winter, they took three days off and were married in Jakarta. Her parents sent a hundred dollars—probably their vacation money—and Jay's father, a cultural affairs officer with the State Department, wired them twenty-five through the embassy.

They returned to their assignments, still seeing each other only one day a week, until, at the end of the tour, they took a four-day honeymoon in Bali. It was the first time they had been together knowing they would not be separating.

Which may have accounted for their first deep uneasiness with each other. *He didn't know what marriage would mean,* she wrote in the diary.

Even less than most people. Companionship itself is hard for him. He didn't go into the Corps for adventure, or idealism, or experience. He went in to be a foreigner, the way he was when he grew up. He was escaping intimacy; then he was trapped by it. Maybe he opened to me in Java because I was a foreigner too. Of course, he needed me physically.

Like many secretive, baffled men, Jay was an extraordinarily intense lover. He relished the depths and special silence of the sexual waters. Love-making was his release and his attainment. He was a generous lover. Only during exam weeks did he lose sight of her. Then he labored grimly in her body to unlock himself for his work.

He never talked about sex. It was one of the first things that turned him against her new friends. When she told him what they'd told her about their amorous problems, he said the reason they had problems was that "they liked problems more than love and they think frankness certifies authenticity. Nothing is more of a disguise than that kind of openness."

"I don't see how honesty can be dishonest."

"Too much light blinds. Those who feel love can't talk about it."

She was unwilling to certify this self-praise. He was not malicious; he had the assertiveness of those who fear uncertainty. Why make him still more uncertain? "I passed your pal Vanessa in the library. She was chattering like a maniac. Why is she so noisy? To convince herself she exists? There ought to be a bank for shallowness. Your pals could deposit their daily slivers of self. After a few years, they might have enough for a genuine moment or two."

"I think they're genuine."

"You have a certain solidity which gets reflected in them. You supply what you think you see in them."

Even for this rare compliment, she could not betray her friends. "I wish I had enough for myself, let alone to pass around."

At first, her friends said he was beautiful. Then they decided there was something wrong in his looks: not the features, not the snow and strawberry complexion, or—when they knew her better—"that beautiful tight ass." Maybe the eyes, which looked "like mud with fog caught in it," said Wanda, or the extra centimeters of forehead, which always caught light. "That portable nimbus of his. What a strange saint."

What really got them was his distance, his conspicuous restraint. Wanda said he looked at them as if they were sick and he the only available suppository—"one that isn't all that happy about being inserted."

Jay converted them into caricatures: Wanda was "Mount Fat," Clover Callahan was "Mouse," Vanessa was "the Tongue," and Nora, who had nothing on which he could fix, became his own incapacity to fix her, "the Slitherer."

"What's that mean?"

"She has no fixity. It's why clothes are so important to her."

"They are to me too. I just don't have anything to spend on them."

"It's different. She has nothing underneath. She's a flag without a country. She's slither. The Guccied Slitherer." Proclaimed with a discoverer's triumph.

"And you're the Archimedes of slander," said Hanna, but under her breath.

Still, abuse was better than silence. Most nights, silence piled around her. It was like the first months in Java, except that there she knew her tour would come to an end. Jay would study five or six hours without saying anything. Or he would call out, "Why are there no apples?" in such despair that the question was almost metaphysical—amazement at nature's astonishing omission of such an item.

Jay would not discuss their relationship. "It works or it doesn't. Ours mostly works. Discussion kills." He pointed across the Midway to the Gothic stretch of the university.

67

"There's discussion for you. The mausoleum of the real."

The most assiduous of graduate students, never missing a class or an assignment, he hated the idea of the university. "For scholars, the world exists in order to be explained," he explained. He hated anthropology, his field, its "patronizing tolerance." Morgan, a young assistant professor, *la plus noire* of his *bêtes noires*, had made fun of the green revolution. "Of those thousands of hours you and I put into the paddies. Because the new seeds require petrochemical fertilizers and oil prices are ruining them. As if we were responsible for oil prices. The world's just a collection of props for his notions, mutters his structuralist honey while eighteen mammary glands quiver at him. What are we doing here, baby? Five hundred million people turn into compost while we pay thousands to listen to theoretical snot."

Jay had grown up inside the coziness which compensates foreign service officers for living abroad. He had lain on a couch while a servant five times his age bent down to serve him iced drinks. At prep school, back in the States, he'd turned against his class. His senior honors thesis on American writers was a fiery tract.

Like Henry James, who wrote "Everything costs that one does for the rich," Fitzgerald saw the rich up close, saw the murder in their charm, their totalitarian need to wipe out individuality and talent. All great American writers have known that, the Hemingway of A Moveable Feast, *the Melville who created in Captain Ahab the warning not to convert nature into commodity.*

The headmaster had written an amused alert to Jay's parents: "One of our brightest boys, though he needs more steering than we've been able to supply. Maybe Stanford will do better." But Jay's parents were pleased with him; his visits to them in Brussels or Karachi were affectionate and brief. He visited less often while he was in college. When his mother died in Bangkok, he wrote his father that he would attend a private service, he didn't have to travel around the world to mourn her. Hanna, thinking of this, wondered when "love had died in him."

Does he love me? Do I love him? I don't know. Know only that my world is too jayed. *I used to be confident, happy. If I had to draw myself now, I would draw a zero. Except zero's useful.*

2

"I don't see why you miss the jungle," said Jay. "You've got your pals."

There was something in it. Her friends were messed up, and somehow overgrown. Each day she saw how troubled they were.

Clover, Wanda, and Vanessa suffered terribly. Yet they were remarkable, gifted girls.

Clover was a math whiz who'd published a paper on set theory as a college sophomore ten years ago.

Wanda was a physical monster with Leonardo-like gifts: she sculpted, embroidered, made furniture, repaired watches, radios, toilets, played the guitar, painted, made beautiful lithographs.

Vanessa couldn't look a dog in the eye, but in class she scorched inferior analysis, and leaped from language to language as if Babel had never been. The intellectual blaze burned connectives from her speech; she spoke a code it took months getting used to. In the Grotto, where they met for lunch, she felt less pressure. The light, submarine and bluish, did not make her feel "on stage"; she was coherent, fluent, sympathetic. Her talk, all their talk, wound in and out of anger, bafflement, flight, odium, fear, and disguise, but its mode was farce. They sat in a corner on facing benches eating thick, meaty soups and talking out each other's troubles. Trouble was their subject, their poetry.

Clover would have been beautiful except for a dermal scurf that was the façade of a wintry interior. Until a breakthrough in her analysis, she had thought of men as statues, dignified and untouchable, women as sluttish hunks, stuff for centerfolds. With the analyst's help, she was able to see the relationship between such distortion and her anorexia: she'd starved herself in order to make her flesh disappear. At eighty pounds, she felt monstrous, overblown. The year before, she'd nearly starved to death. Influenza saved her life; she'd gone in for a flu shot and was put in the hospital. Now, stronger, she could see, literally see, that women were worthy and men approachable. Although she still sometimes felt like "a pea in an invisible pod," she also believed in herself and even hoped for some kind of physical relationship with someone. "I used to have nothing but numbers. A freak, like someone who can whistle with her knees."

Mathematics was not her only gift. She had an extraordinary sense for other people's suffering. "She knows before you do," said Vanessa. "It's like the sixth sense some animals have for warmblooded creatures." Clover was always on call. People who didn't know her well telephoned at midnight, and she went to talk them back to life.

Wanda's trouble lay under more layers than Troy; enormous energy piled fat, wit, manual genius, and a sense of spectacle over it. Caped to the throat, hair in a great bush, Wanda was the center of any room. She had a lovely, subtle voice which spun the gossip of Hyde Park into

70

manic catastrophes. No one had ever been in Wanda's rooms, though she told Clover—who told Hanna—that she had an intimate friend there. No particulars. (Jay said Wanda had only personified a layer of fat.)

Vanessa was married to a biologist who was driven wild by her hypomania. She knew it, was helpless with the knowledge and the condition. "Knowing, doing, different kettles, different fish." Vanessa had a beautiful body, a harsh, ugly face, tiny nosed, huge lipped. Her husband was handsome, and she was terrified of losing him, but driving him away was better than being left by him. She showed him up, interrupted him, read papers which challenged his—and hated herself. She lived on Valium, had nightmares so awful that after them she'd come close to killing herself.

Compared to the other girls, Nora and Hanna were untroubled. They'd been loved, embraced, encouraged. The Grotto patrons took them for sisters. Both were tall and had dark hair which fell over their shoulders. Nora's was thicker and more lustrous; when she was nervous, her hands ran through it.

Nora's small troubles came from excess: she did lots of things well, painted, wrote poetry, was a good athlete—she ran two miles a day at the gym—did honors work in Romance languages. But she was terrified of criticism, and ran away before it came. Her plan was to finish her master's and become a talk-show hostess. "Hard questions are easy to ask. And Barbara Walters is wearing out." She was also looking into government internships, law school, Vista, Fulbrights to Guatemala, museum training courses, the Sarasota Clown School. "Why not? I love the circus." No notion outlasted the required follow-up.

Her love life was equally serial. She'd lived with eight or

ten boys since she'd been in school, the last a "beautiful Nigerian" who'd finished an economics degree and just left to work for OPEC. "It's a relief to lose him. He was heading so straight for the future, he could hardly remember where we lived."

"I envy that," said Hanna.

"I envy you. You've got the toughest decisions behind you."

Hanna said it wasn't so at all, and told her how she'd become a prisoner of Jay's moroseness. "He's dear, but he hates life. It's impossible to reach him."

Nora said every relationship with a man had more censorship than expression. "The sex is so important, you sacrifice give-and-take for it."

Hanna said that wasn't what she feared. She did fear Jay. "He's never laid a finger on me, but I'm afraid of him. Physically afraid. Anger's burned the fat off his bones, and I think it has nowhere to go now but on mine. It's not just a few knocks. I'm not that afraid of pain. It's the anger itself. I guess I shouldn't say it. I love him, he's remarkable in his way. But to be squeezed so is awful. To feel your nature so reduced. I'd always hoped marriage would give me space, energy, desire. It hasn't."

"Try getting out of it more. Don't bury yourself in him. He's become your tomb. Get out. On your own." Nora told her to come over for supper, Jay could manage without her. "It would be the first time," said Hanna.

"She didn't invite *me?*"

Jay was assembling the evening's fortress: apples, books, ballpoints, the vaseful of Sanka.

"She thinks I ought to get out on my own once in a while."

Troubles

"Fine. Just don't come back on a broomstick."

"Meaning?"

The long face tilted, peering over a celestial ledge. "Witchery's contagious."

"Nora's no witch."

"Wait till midnight. I stood behind what's-her-name, Mount Fuji, the one that sounds like a stray. Wanda! In the Co-op. She was adding her groceries on a pocket calculator. Batting her pig eyes. Not at me. The groceries. Six bags full. And none for my master, or for any dame but you know who. At least the Slitherer has a streak of generosity in her."

"You and I don't exactly keep a great salon."

"All we're trying to do is get out of here quick as we can. We're not the Salvation Army."

"I don't mean to criticize," she said.

"I don't know what you mean."

"It's been my fault too. Our life's too airless. The girls have been a fine thing for me. I feel human with them. You pick at them. I know it's a kind of game for you, your way of being social with me, but sometimes it's too hard."

He opened a book, looked at it, drank from the vase. "OK. I won't say anything about them. If I have an opinion you don't share, I'll shut up. But Hanna, I can't have those psychotic shrews around here. Sorry."

That night, asleep beside him, she dreamed she was at the top of the Buddhist mountain, Boroboudur. Out of the stone bells rose old teachers, her sister, her mother, a boyfriend from Oklahoma who had hit her for not making out with him, girls from grade school and high school. One by one they asked her to forgive them. "We're sorry, we didn't know." *"Mai ben rai,"* she said. "Never mind"—and then was ashamed, for it was Thai, not Javanese. Which

73

brought her to a river, a kayak going down the klongs. Jay lay dead on the struts, the boat headed for the cremation pyre. She was crying. "The others' don't mean anything without yours," she said, meaning the petitions for forgiveness, and now she would never have his. The body moved next to her. Jay. She moved away. In the channel between sleep and waking, she knew she was going to leave him.

3

The next night, before Jay got home, Hanna left a note for him and walked across the Midway to Nora's. She'd taken a shower, and put on her best jeans, an openwork blouse over a bra that lifted her breasts, and a blue blazer that was the nicest thing she owned.

Nora lived on Dorchester in a large attic room with a kitchen off one side and a bathroom off another. The furniture consisted of mattresses covered with shawls and cushions. There were lots of plants, books, a stereo, and knickknacks. The walls were covered with prints of Matisse flowers and dancers.

Nora, barefoot, wore old jeans and a sweater.

"You look terrific," she said. "Like someone on vacation."

"Going out to dinner is vacation. Without Jay."

They had jasmine tea, and faced each other on the mattresses. Through old blinds, sun dusted the room.

"Are you on probation?" Nora's hands ran in and out of her hair.

"It's more like I've dug my way out of a cell. Blind. Through muck."

74

"No mud shows."

"The mud's in here," said Hanna, touching her left breast.

"That's nice mud," said Nora.

There was something both tense and easy in this pillowed room, a Turkish air. Hanna felt airy, afloat, yet cloistered, marooned. "I feel high."

"Free," said Nora. "Or maybe hungry. You hungry?"

"Just for air."

"It'll have to be tea."

Hanna brought her cup to the stove. Nora looked at her, her eyes, then her blouse, and put an arm around her waist. Hanna put hers around Nora's shoulder. They leaned forward and kissed.

Nora undid Hanna's blouse and bra. Undressed, they lay down, looked at and stroked each other, then, aroused, became more intimate.

It was, thought Hanna, like making love to oneself. There was the sense that Nora knew her body from inside. It wasn't especially exciting. It was almost a form of reconnaissance. Nora, no stranger in this country, was able to go further.

To be companionable, Hanna pretended thorough satisfaction.

4

It was midnight when Nora drove her back. Jay had read her note, which told him to read her diary so that he could understand how troubled she was by their marriage.

"I don't think I can live with you," said the note. "Not

now. It doesn't mean I don't love you. Whatever that big word means."

Jay read the diary, more and more infuriated by what he regarded as its insensitivity. "Why couldn't she have opened up to me? It's those damn creeps. She had to find something, to keep up with them. If they're not in a mess, they don't know they're alive. Is life supposed to be paradise?"

He found a few dollars and ran down to the all-night liquor store on 63rd Street, bought a quart of vodka, and by midnight had drunk half of it.

Hanna came upstairs and saw him marooned in his sad, magic circle (the silvery bottle filling in for the vase of Sanka). "Well?"

"I'm potted."

"You read the note?"

"You bet."

"And the diary?"

"I followed all instructions."

He sat in liquorousness like a fish in an aquarium— apparently the same, but altered by the tiny ambience of his new situation (of which the booze was but an element). Yet he looked beautiful, wounded, extravagant, baffled, and—to her surprise, for she'd had some experience of liquor—sexually excited. Even more surprising, she felt a responsive excitement. The signals crossed; discussion was shunted to the side.

For the second time that evening, she took off her clothes. They did not even bother to go down the hall but made love on the floor beside the apple cores and vodka.

Yet, Hanna told herself, half an hour later, awake while he snoozed off beyond troubles, she was in the jungle with Vanessa and Wanda and Clover. Energy, talent and hope

Troubles

warred with her life; no relationship and no institution could help. She had the isolation of a pioneer in the circumstance of a soap opera. The only ax she had was the knowledge she was in trouble, that she was down there with the others.

Lesson for the Day

Kiest, with lots of time on his hands—his wife had a job, he didn't—had fallen for—that is, couldn't wait to get in the sack with—Angela Deschay, a pie-eyed, soft-voiced, long-legged, frizzily gorgeous assistant professor in his wife Dottie's department. Dottie and Angela were soaring together. It was WE—Woman's Era—in the universities. Every department had to account to Equal Opportunity Boards in the University and in Washington for its minority hiring practices. Humanities departments had long since run out of qualified blacks and Chicanos, the few in these fields were more precious than natural gas strikes. But there were still good supplies of women. "Not enough to have a representative or two," rumbled Kiest. "You have to represent the whole miserable spectrum, pouters, grinners, thumpers, grunts. And then you can't fire'm. Fire a slit"—he'd borrowed that term from the misogynist, Ty

Cobb—"and you've got a fire on your hands. They get a new job Wednesday and sue you for the one they lost Tuesday. Lost purposely, so they can collect double."

The rumbling went on, mostly to himself or to his three- and one-year-old sons who did not exactly tune in to it. It was just Dad going on.

What else did he have to do? He'd been done out of his place by the world's women. In fact, it was Angela Deschay who filled the slot he'd have filled here in Madison. The slit in the slot. His lust for her had been blocked and then ignited by the injustice.

"What leg can a man stand on?" This to Dottie over the repulsive Cheerios he bought—of course he did the shopping—because she detested them. "The one in the middle? That's the one that does us in." Thin, bespectacled, mild and innocent-looking despite his rage, Kiest threatened her with transsexual operations. On her, on himself. "I'll turn slit and give you a run for our money."

Would she even notice? She rushed off, she rushed in, flew to conferences, interviewed, was interviewed, formed and chaired committees, got job offers, salary raises. At this publication-insistent university, her only post-dissertation work was a bloody attack on her own dissertation adviser's swan-song book on George Herbert. (So veiled with fulsome praise that only Kiest and the victim knew what went on. Dottie herself didn't know. Her aggression was just hearty instructiveness. "He wouldn't respect me if I didn't point out a few things. He's the last man to want friendship to shackle scholarship.") The tigerish assault was pronounced "brilliant" by senior professors who otherwise couldn't justify Dottie's unstoppable rise.

Kiest foresaw their life: Dottie as Chairperson, Dean, Provost, President; board directorships, a cabinet post, and

who knows then? He would be Henry Lucing it after her—
with the difference that Henry Luce had been Henry Luce,
whereas he had never been allowed to be more than just
Kiest.

What had he done? Well, he'd written a dissertation on
the great and terrible John Wilmot, Earl of Rochester. At
graduate school, he'd done far better than Dottie, and yet
he could not find a job within a hundred miles of hers.
She'd been wined, dined, grabbed for, prostrated before,
you'd have thought she was a fusion of Madame Curie and
Marilyn Monroe. She was only an enthusiast, a worker, a
prettyish, big-bottomed, straitlaced, no, slightly unlaced
girl out of the bleached Calvinism of Dutch Reform
Michigan. They'd met at the Yale Graduate School, drawn
together in dislike of the critical virtuosi there. The literary
pantheon at Yale didn't feature Shakespeare, Milton and
Wordsworth but the versions of them offered by H. Miller,
H. Bloom, G. Hartman and S. Fish (whom Kiest rebap-
tized as Grinder, Wither, Thrombosis and Carp). Each
day, he and Dottie watched them lash, hash and hack *Lear,*
Comus, Browning and Blake into puzzles of hamburger.
"The texts we live and die by," said young Kiest. "And
over in Romance, the Barthes-Derrida swine are fusion-
bombing Balzac and Stendhal. Who'd dare to write a
poem in New Haven?"

Not Kiest. It had never been his ambition. All he'd
wanted was a chance to dig into the grand old texts. There
were plenty of first-rate meals to be made out of those
ingredients.

Dottie was saved by languages. At Olivet, she'd majored
in classics; at Yale, this was her redoubt, a pocket of
antique resistance to the critical buzz-bombs. Fresh-faced,
pop-eyes agleam with untouched availability, she wrote the

thick, paratactic, unnecessary-to-read prose that was called wonderful writing in the academy.

He, Kiest, had come out of the Garden District of New Orleans with ever-thinning Southern speech. His father had been pastry chef at the Commodore Palace Hotel, he became an early observer, then a master of aristocratic ways. Adolescent, he found the bookstores in the Quarter, and by senior year was enough ahead of his classmates to win a fellowship—"they'll change it to 'pal-ship'"—to Tulane, and after that, a fatter one to Yale. Ascent was written all over him. Dottie, with innocent hunger, grabbed him. How could she know she'd grabbed a lemon?

Or did she? Had she known even then she'd need a Kiest at home for kids, for chores? He wasn't sure. He accused her of *uni-sexing* him. Even then, she knew both the unimportance and the necessity of his complaints. She'd become one of the least passionate twenty-eight-year-olds in America, but, in complaint-time, she could slide into brilliant sexual parody, so that tumbling on her pale rear, or bouncing the bud-nippled chest, complaint melted away. Being home so much did fierce things to the sexual appetite.

Which is how Angela Deschay filled his head.

The Deschays lived across the grassy street. Angela too was a rising star, not in administration, but scholarship. She published complex articles on Revenge, Power-Hunger, Persiflage and Dominance in Restoration Comedy. Before she'd come to Madison, she'd looked up Kiest's dissertation (thinking that the *Kiest* on the roster was Mervyn L., not Dorothy M.). They were on the same intellectual frequency. Her husband, Jimmy, was in the Divinity School, one of the hip new preachers, full of pop cultural garbage spaced tediously by spiritous infusion of

Lesson for the Day

Barth and Bultmann, Troeltsch and Tillich. Eyeglassed, helpful, huge, eager, Jimmy was full of soft causes, soft politics and frequent soft furies which exhausted, sometimes paralyzed him. "How could she have married him?" groaned Kiest to little Myron, Baby Dan. Madisonians—he knew—asked the same question about Dottie.

He and Angela walked their kids along the lake and talked about the seventeenth century, university politics and, after a few awkward skirmishes, sex and marriage. She knew his views deeply, they were in his dissertation. Kiest spelled out his own failure in Rochester's. The bitter entertainer, pimp and jester to the monstrous king, was a rioter, hater, débauché, an actor and counterfeiter who disguised himself as tramp, porter, mountebank doctor. Hobbesian apostle and poet of Nothing, Rochester knew that the difference between con-man and banker was that the banker's credit lasted one day longer; that coward and hero differed because the day the coward had to put up, the hero didn't. His couplets lashed everyone from crowned king to two-crown strumpet. Age thirty-three, burnt out by japes, revels, punks, liquor and disbelief, he was converted by Bishop Burnet, and died in the arms of wife, children, debts and church.

Kiest, five years shy of Rochester's deathbed age, had had no king, only dream queens, no career of make-believe, only a non-career of it. His debauches were oneiric. Home, after a first springday stroll by the sail-white, passionate lake, he put the kids down for naps and took out the two hundred and forty bound pages of his dissertation, *Rochester, The Burning Counterfeit*. Its harsh prose seemed beautiful to him, he mouthed the great Earl's poems. Angela's legs and breasts, her thick-glassed green eyes, mop of twiny, glittery, leafgold hair, her long back with—

surely—its generous dip into the beauteous twins, oh what a woman.

> Naked she lay, claspt in my longing arms,
> I filled with love, and she all over charms,
> Both equally inspired with eager fire,
> Melting through kindness, flaming in desire.

For all her dutiful distance and careful amiability, Angela—he was sure—burned for him. She was the right age, the hot late twenties, and she'd seen around, through and over her hefty, dull divine.

> With arms, legs, lips close clinging to embrace,
> She clips me to her breast, and sucks me to her face.

Angela, Jesus, Mary.

> The nimble tongue (love's lesser lightning) played
> Within my mouth, and to my thoughts conveyed
> Swift orders, that I should prepare to throw
> The all-dissolving thunderbolt below.

Kiest turned on the bed, piled pillows stiff with Sears' floral print into an Angelac body.

> In liquid raptures I dissolve all o'er
> Melt into sperm and spend at every pore.
> A touch from any part of her had done 't,
> Her hand, her foot, her very looks a c . . t.

Don't.

Lips on pillow, Angela's, and more, more. Other women. Dottie. Angela and Dottie together, hugging, kissing, grinding into porno flicks. His weapon, abused on the rough florets, clumped with generative sap. Window light poured rebuke: "So, Kiest, this is your career. What a great man you are. Life seized by the throat. Another great day, Kiest. Sculptors are itching to get you down in bronze."

Jimmy Deschay was making his preaching debut. More final exam than ministerial vocative, but no matter, it was a large event, and the Kiests were asked to swell the congregation that was part of it. The sacred tryout was in the First Methodist Church of Springvale, twelve miles west of Madison, fifty feet off the Interstate. Kids had been bunched with a single baby-sitter. Kiest drove the Deschays' nine-year-old Dodge Dart, sitting beside Jimmy, whose terror dominated fierce silence. The preacher's hands were in and out of his hair, cut into shaggy bangs like Robespierre's. (Every few months, he adopted another antique revolutionary style: ponytailed like young Jefferson, curled like Simon Bolivar.) His eye-sockets, lips and chin-cleft dripped; cheekbones, forehead and chocolate-kiss eyes shone liquidly. The radiant April Sunday darkened in the car. Dottie made talk but was shushed by the Lord's frightened bridegroom. Angela, bareheaded, jouncy in her orange-flower dress, tried comfort and was likewise shushed. Jimmy needed all lines clear for late words from on high.

"Is he trying to drum messages from his scalp?" thought Kiest, furious at Jimmy's contagious frenzy. "That great Vidal Sassoon in the sky? Damn sheepish shepherd."

In church, he sat between the ladies. What a position. Never, never had human appendages so moved him. Under the flocculent orange balls bent the superb, un-stockinged, untanned legs of this scholarly charmer, this—

85

please God—sluttish slit. They straightened for hymns, for prayers, up, down, arms, sides, raising and lowering hymnals, fifty, seventy small contacts. She knew, surely, the warmth he generated, the feel of his suit sleeve, the tensed communication of his arm. The holy place, the holy occasion covered the awareness with unthinkability. "But," thought Kiest, "She is thinking. She *knows.*"

> Rise up, oh men of God.
> Have done with lesser things.

No music reader, Kiest fumbled toward the notes behind Dottie's authority, Angela's warble. Hymnals bounced to the thin tune, hymn-booked arms rocked, parted, touched. Down they sat, arms and sides sending and receiving.

"Here we go," thunder-whispered Dottie.

Jimmy was up, black-robed, huge. Sheets of light spread from the great windows over sixty worshipers. An electric moment. "Dear friends," dove Jimmy. "The lesson for the day is Matthew 26. 23. 'And he answered and said, He that dippeth his hand with me in the dish, the same shall betray me.'"

"Mother Mary. Does the bastard know?"

Kiest's thought was not just his. Air spiked between his sleeve and the bare arm beside it. The power of words.

"God," said Dottie. "Something's wrong."

The ministerial tower tilted. From the top, vowels bassooned into each other, "Aarch, eeech, uuueeeshhh." Black wings rose, sank, rose; the left wiped the ministerial brow.

"Jimmy." Angela, hands fisted, sent useless strength his way. "Oh please."

Whereupon, not God but Kiest came to the rescue.

Lesson for the Day

Small and straight, he walked the little nave and joined the stunned divine. Jimmy's face, red as if strangled, widened fishily. "Mr. Deschay," said Kiest to the assembly, "rose from a sickbed against his doctor's warning in order to preach today. It's clear he shouldn't have. With his permission, and yours, I'll read his sermon for him."

The colors of humiliation and terror countered those of surprise, relief. Jimmy touched the shoulder of his substitute, then sent the flock those eloquent gestures which would in future decades be seen in the smaller congregations of southern North Dakota. Back in his seat, hands folded, he gave perfect attention, as if he were the benign appraiser of his rescuer.

Kiest looked at the typescript and gave it his fervent all. "Is this betrayal story the essence of Jesus's last Passover? I think not. Grand as the grand story is, deep as it touches our sense of fair play, the betrayal, necessary prelude to the great sacrifice, is not the ultimate meaning. No, dear friends." His eyes found the thick glass behind which were the astonished, excited, decision-taking green eyes of the stricken fledgling's wife. Rescued from her own sympathy and humiliation less by Kiest's stunning move than by the moronic complacence with which her bedmate accepted it, she showed in her look an invigorated sense of the author of *Rochester, The Burning Counterfeit*. And sure enough, pondering this new acquaintance, she heard clear substitution in the laborious text: lines from the wicked Earl's "Satire Against Mankind," surely never before or after heard from this pulpit.

Birds feed on birds, beasts on each other prey,
But savage Man alone does Man betray.
Pressed by necessity, *they* kill for food,

Man undoes Man to do himself no good . . .
For fear he arms, and is of arms afraid;
From fear to fear successively betrayed.
Base fear the source whence his best passions came,
His boasted honor and his dear-bought fame . . .

"So," said Kiest over nodding, scratching, shaking heads, "as Reverend Deschay tells us, the betrayal in the midst of the celebrating feast is the essential savagery of man which, in hours, Jesus will die to redeem. So, on this second Sunday after Easter, do not lose yourself in the savage ecstasy of spring, fine as it may be"—small, wild rustling below—"without remembering that amidst your feasting self the unredeemed beast trembles in readiness. And here Reverend Deschay bids you turn to Number 29 in the hymnal, 'There is a land of pure delight where saints immortal reign.'"

That evening, while Dottie was out with her Sunday play-reading group—playing Regina in *Another Part of the Forest*—Kiest put his sons to bed, and then from his door sill, sent brainwaves of imploration across the forty feet of grass to Angela.

Surely she'd managed to drug her preacher into sleep. The ass had covered his debacle with Kiest's excuse for it; so well had he mimicked chills and fever that he suffered them. The car ride back to Madison had been filled with his sniffles. Kiest and Angela had not looked at each other. That was the sign: she knew; he knew. What more was necessary? Knowledge embraced need, need the invitation to requital. *What was holding her back?*

Gold shadows thickened, purpled. A fat moon sat in the oaks. The lights burned at the Deschays', but that was all.

Lesson for the Day

Kiest's expectation became anxiety, then misery. Ten
o'clock. He threw in the towel and headed for the armistice
of bed.

The phone. "Mervyn," said Angela.

"Thank God."

"No, *you*. Thank *you.*"

"All right, come thank me."

Crucial silence. "Papers."

Papers.

Of course. End of term for the full-time assistant
professor. Wife, mother, assigner of papers, reader of
exams, there was hardly time for sleep, let alone . . . *let
alone.*

"I need, I want, I must." The unuttered conjugation of
Kiest's hunger. He put what he could of it into "Angela."

"Yes, Mervyn." Slowly, softly. It was something. Then,
probably faking, "Coming, Jimmy. Goodbye."

Coming, Jimmy. The counterfeiting slit.

Kiest went into the terrible spring night. The moon
hung in it like an ulcer. *What to do?*

Headlights in the oaks, and a professorial Dodge pulled
to the curb. Dottie. Hot and rosy with self-gratulation:
"Bye-bye. Thanks, again. See you next time. Bye-bye."

Kiest slipped inside, doused the bedlight, took off his
clothes under the blanket, closed his eyes.

"Asleep already, baby?"

"No longer."

"Sorry, lambie. Had to tell you. Zack said he'd do it at
the Repertory if I'd play Regina." Off with the square
slacks, the fuchsia turtleneck. "If I didn't have to chair
that Curriculum Revision." Into the bathroom, front and
rear nakedly abounce, splash, scrub, towel and tinkle, she
never closed the door, and back to the dark bed in her

grim, dust-colored pjs. "What a day." The bedlight shriveled Kiest's eyelids. "Sorry, sweetie, I've got a Special Fields on Coleridge at nine. Won't take me long. 'Frost at Midnight.'"

"You said it."

"Want to hear?" A specialist in metrics who couldn't find an accent with a Saint Bernard, Dottie sometimes treated him to a reading.

Why not? The day had supplied everything else. Coleridge was the one romantic poet he understood from inside: idler, dreamer, opium-guzzler, fragment-heaper, a mothering father, isolated, sex-starved, pent up with the wrong woman, dying for another. "Read on."

But Dottie, racing, underlining, scribbling, was almost done and could only cap this day of counterfeit and despair with the final wintry lines: "'. . . the secret ministry of frost/ Shall hang them up in silent icicles/ Quietly shining to the quiet Moon.'"

Double Charley

Professional deformity: the dyer's hand, the blacksmith's forearm, the model's complexion, the lawyer's skepticism. And the songwriter's?

"Mindlessness," said Charley Schmitter to his longtime collaborator, Charley Rangel. "Empty-mindedness. So your tunes don't bump into anything but my jingles. And vice versa."

Manifestly untrue, but Charley Schmitter never reconciled himself to "this degraded métier." "The Greatness of the American Musical Comedy" was not an admissible topic at Schmitter's table.

On the other hand, Schmitter gave no quarter to *official* poets. "Glue-eyed narcissists, licking the fat off their own bones so some acne-headed sophomore can have his quota of wet dreams. So some Bulgarian history major can think about something while she mouths his member. 'I wan-

91

dered lonely as a cow/That chews the cud of Chairman Mao.' Ohhhh, soobleem.''

Immense, passionate, mad for his own spiels and his own learning, Charley Schmitter couldn't be contained by any métier.

At least, this was the sense of his old-time collaborator. "Soon as he had a few bucks salted away, he could become what he always was, a spieler, a schmooser." This to Maggie Moon, Rangel's off-and-on-again companion. "He's the most profoundly self-contented man in the world." (Rangel himself was no slouch in that department.) "He's got a tolerant, gifted wife, willing tootsies, the constitution of Mount Blanc. And he doesn't need more than ten or twelve thousand bucks a year to pay for his lousy flannel shirts, Gallo Rhine and Egg Foo Yung. The greatest pleasure he provides himself: schmoos. He only calls now to try it out on me. When was the last time I had a lyric out of him? Seven years ago?"

"Too long," said Maggie.

" 'Starved in Fat City.' His last trip out here. Six, seven years ago. Just before your vanishing act."

Afraid that her irregular life was upsetting Chippie, her ten-year-old daughter, Maggie had disappeared one morning, bag and baggage. For three weeks, Rangel had had no word at all. Then a one-line card from New York: "Chippie had to get away. Love, M." (Which, thought Rangel, was the reason he didn't set "Fat City"; never would.)

That had been dark-night-of-the-soul time for him. He'd lived with Maggie five years, since he'd come back to Chicago. There'd been no commissions coming in, jockeys weren't playing their songs. Only now and then would a "Golden Oldies" play a Double Charley. So he came back to the apartment he'd grown up in on West Armitage above the candy store his parents owned. (It was a Christian Science Reading Room now.) Maggie had left her third husband, "the Casanova of cotton goods," and was working in the Billing Office of Roosevelt Hospital. Rangel came in to complain and walked out with an invitation. His own wife had stayed in Santa Monica, was en route to marrying the unit manager of a tv news station. The great sexual switchboard had more kinks than Ma Bell's System, but, sooner or later, everyone got plugged in, if only to his own opening.

Rangel fell so hard for pretty Maggie, he wasn't bothered by her marital record. "I just kept trying. It was a substitute for BA, MA, PhD. I'm an expert now, Charley. And you're—what's that Kern song?—'My Man.'"

"Pollack and Yvain," corrected little Charley.

For the first year, he'd been so charged by her presence in the same apartment, he thought he couldn't think of anything else. It turned out to be the best year he'd had in a decade. Schmitter caught fire and Decca took a flutter on a Double Charley album. (Connoisseurs of the Forties made room for it between their Beatles'.)

A largish girl, especially next to tiny Rangel, Maggie had the complexion of an English milkmaid. Pretty to the point of unreality: a perfect bobbed nose and eyes so strangely lit by every feeling, you could not concentrate on their color— a blue-flecked verdure. When she put on weight—every six months or so—it went to her face and marred the perfection. But such distinctions were only for Maggie and such experts as himself. Passersby still kept looking back for seconds; quite a tribute to a woman docking at fifty.

Back then, though, her beauty and their passion were intensified by what she called "the condiment of guilt."

It was that, she said, that made her take off. Chippie, "disturbed by the irregular life," was stuttering. Rangel told her many children stuttered. "Ignore the stutter, respond to the meaning."

But Maggie, fearful of imperfection, rushed the little girl. "Speak up, speak up." Of course, it got worse. Rangel begged, ordered, threatened. For him, children were sacred. "The look on Chippie when she tries to get a sentence out," he told Schmitter, who'd come to Chicago for a work week. "It breaks me, Charley. I never hit a woman in my life, let alone the one I loved. But if she gets on that kid again, I may break her nose."

Did that message reach Maggie? In any case, within a week, she and Chippie were off.

A month later, Schmitter telephoned to say he'd seen her, she was working in the Billing Office at Lenox Hill. "Seems to be all right, Charley."

"I don't care," Rangel had said. "If it weren't for Chippie, I'd hire a truck to break her bones. Every part of me that loved her hates her. But I've even stopped dreaming of busting her nose. God bless whatever physics does it."

Ten months later, he saw her in the Art Institute. "I don't believe it." She was gaunt, newly beautiful. "Why didn't you call me?"

"I thought you'd kill me."

She'd been back two months, had an apartment in Hyde Park with a librarian at IIT, Olive Baum. She worked in the Billing Office at Michael Reese. Chippie was at Kenwood, a good public school.

They began going out again, and then, after a visit from Schmitter and the consequent departure of Olive Baum,

94

Double Charley

she and Chippie came back to West Armitage. Stutter
gone, Chippie went to Francis Parker; Rangel paid.

"It's like leaves," Rangel told Schmitter between spiels.
"Once the chlorophyll factories start churning out all that
green, you can't see those gorgeous reds that'll kill them in
the fall. She's back, we click, she's for me, it's green for
go."

"Not bad, little Charley. Maybe I can work it up for us."

Rangel knew better than that. There'd be no more lyrics
coming his way. Only happiness with Maggie eased the
pain of it then.

"Why can't you write your own?" Maggie asked him.

"Did Gershwin? Did Rodgers?"

"How about Porter? Berlin?"

"I don't have it. I can't even work with anyone but
Charley."

"It's not too late for that. Get the right tune in his head,
push him with a title. Recerebrate him. And you'll have
another Double Charley."

Not that easy.

Though every morning, breaking from sleep, ideas
dribbled into Rangel's head. Sometimes he got them on the
pad beside his reading light. Phrases, rhythms; six bars,
eight. The piano sideboard piled with notecards, ideas
enough for a Ring cycle. But songs themselves, finished
songs, that was something else. He couldn't work without
Schmitter. Didn't know why. After Hart's death, Rodgers
found Hammerstein. Weill had Kaiser, before, Anderson
and a host of others after Brecht. Mercer, Arlen, Youmans,
almost everyone moved from lyric bed to lyric bed.
Without difficulty, nostalgia or remorse. Only he seemed
yoked to one writer. "I'm just a standard thirty-two-bar

Richard Stern

hack," went his self-deprecating line. "Charley's stuff
transfigures me. Without it, I'm dry-gulched. No charge in
the battery. Pffft."

Maggie's suggestion was "Try a new style. It's not you
that's yoked to Charley. It's your old success. You're yoked
to it and call it 'Schmitter.'"

"Anyone else say that, I'd punch his nose. 'Success!' I
hate those damn songs of ours. I hear one on the radio, off
it goes. Antiques. Claptrap. Unbearable. But I can't feel
my way into this new stuff. It sounds like recitative to me.
Sprechstimme. And not such brilliant *Sprech* at that. As for
the seventy-eight varieties of rock, they're demolition
derbies for me. Lyric fission."

Not quite. Rangel was tempted again and again by the
easy speech—"Nim Chimsky could sing it"—the unpush-
iness of the melodic line. "Into you before you know you've
bitten it. But I can't feel it. Can't write it. It's not my line."

From New York, Schmitter telephoned bulletins of self-
gratulation. "We're still a name at the Capers Club.
Frunz"—their longtime agent who now took ten weeks to
answer Rangel's letters—"overheard Steve Keith bawling
out his latest jailbait the other night for not knowing who
Double Charley was. Told her to listen to 'Slit Throat' if
she wanted to know what a song was."

"Did he tell her he lifted six bars from 'Eat This
Heart'?"

"That was flattery too, Charley, you know that." The
telephone magnified Schmitter's wavery treble (a surprise
for those who knew its immense source). "Did Beethoven
sue Schubert for stealing from the 'Kreutzer'?"

"He was dead. Or maybe it killed him. I'da bloodied the
little shit's nostrils."

"Nonsense, sweetheart. It's *noblesse oblige*. Keith has

96

nothing to gain from puffing us. The point is, among cognoscenti, we *still count.*"

"He's made four hundred grand from our six bars, he can afford to pamper his guilt. He probably saw Frunz lapping it up in the corner, knew it would get back to us. More points for Keith."

"Bitter, Charley, bitter."

Why not? Could he live on third-hand compliments? Day after day, he was at the piano, music paper on the flowerless wooden trellis, notes making their way from keys to paper; where they died. In the wordless, the Schmitter-less vacuum, they died. And nothing came from New York. "It's that cretinous broad you introduced him to," he said to Maggie. "She's dried him out. He always said he couldn't work around idiots. And now he pours himself into that mental Sahara."

"She's the sign of his trouble, not the cause. Charley's not young, lambie."

"Sure he is. At ninety, he'll have more sexual charm than Paul Newman. Bulk, bad leg, bronchitis, nothing derails Charley. Age is just a rumor to him. Sickness is for other guys. Stupidity. That's what kills him. He goes home to Agnes to get Olive's stupidity washed off him. I'd finance some babe through a doctorate if she'd play with Charley. He has to have his toke of baby nookie. Look at him."

Pointing. On the wall, in a mosaic frame, was Agnes's marvelous miniature of him. Agnes painted on enamel in the manner of the Persians and Léonard Limosin. Her portrait of Charley had won a prize in Paris. Before that, Rangel had told her he couldn't live without it, and he bought it on time, two hundred dollars a month for four years. There was the great black bramble of a head, the wild mustache ambling into the regal cheeks, Schmitter's bulk jutting over the enamel curve. Beside the figure in the six square inches, a fountain frothed minuscule lilac spray in solar glitter.

That such Flemish genius flowed from the florid, muscular, eagle-browed Agnes had been an art world secret for decades. Only with the Paris exhibition in the mid-Sixties did Agnes Schmitter become the name behind those few, tiny works of refined genius. Till then, she was only what she kept on being, Charley Schmitter's passionate, tolerant, quarrelsome, adoring, bellicose worshiper. For years, she'd shut her eyes to the passionate geniality which poured sexual charm over New York ladies.

Not that Charley ever *came on*. He was just there, waiting with a rub here, a kiss there. His parts bulged in his corduroys. Of them, and anything else that was not controlled by the power of thought, he was magnificently careless. What counted was mental power. "It's why I work with Rangel," he'd said from the beginning. "Not just that he's a top musician. He could be twice as good, and I wouldn't work with him if he were a dope."

Maggie kept telling Rangel Schmitter would revive. "One day, you'll sing him a few bars, it'll be like a quarter in the juke box. The machinery will crank up again. Olive or no Olive."

Rangel knew it was over, but possibility nagged at him until the last day.

That occurred one month after Charley's last telephonic burst of schmoos. He'd been, he said, reading the poet Jules Laforgue, "the kid Eliot stole the line about measuring out his life with coffee spoons from. Listen to this." And the wavery voice, tinier than ever, read in what seemed to Rangel perfect French, a few difficult lines of verse.

98

Double Charley

"'Divers Flutes!' How does that enchant you? 'Mademoiselle who might have wished to hear the wood of my diversity of flutes display themselves a bit.' Can you imagine crooning that to a hundred, a hundred million people? And that's the source of modern mentality as they see it at Cambridge and the Sorbonne. Think Stockhausen could work up a tune for that baby?

"I'm glad we never worked that side of the street. That's for No-One-Caresville. We're down where people eat, sleep, love and die. In tune with *this* world. We didn't go diving into waterless pools."

On the way to New York for the funeral, Rangel realized that had been Charley's memorial; and—who knows?—perhaps his justification for turning off the spigot while his partner still thirsted.

Two hours before the funeral, Olive Baum called him. (Maggie had given her his number.) She wanted a favor. "Agnes wouldn't let me see him at the hospital." She was crying. "He *wanted* to see me. She *told* me. She had the nerve to tell me. He couldn't speak, could only move his eyelids; and he blinked 'yes' when she asked him if he wanted to see me. She said she asked him twice, and he blinked 'yes,' and she didn't tell me till he was gone. And now she won't tell me where he's being buried. You tell me, please, Charley. You know we loved each other."

"I'll get her to let me tell you, Olive."

Rangel had identified the body for Campbell's; Agnes had been too distraught. In the coffin, ready to go, Charley was de-Schmittered: powdery, Roman, the black bramble head too grand for the wispy neck and the timid blue tie someone had put on him.

The funeral day was rough with January light. An icy

99

day. Tiny Charley sat beside Agnes in the back of the limousine. (He'd always felt smaller next to her than he did next to Charley.) Her face was full of aquiline rancor, her black hair—"I suppose she's dyed it for years"—lay heavily on her shoulders. It smelled musty, sad. The limousine went up the West Side highway heading for Mount of Hope Cemetery. To their surprise, Charley, great scorner of death, had, for forty years, maintained a plot there.

In the mortuary city, his coffin lay on the iced earth among the small gravestones. Below were the grander slabs, one-room marble mansions. While they stood, uncertain what to do, it began to sleet. Drops pelted the coffin. "Should have brought a Bible," said Rangel. "Or an anthology." No poems came to mind. He tried to think of a line from one of their songs. Couldn't. "I guess this is it, kid," he said. "God bless you."

With the soft sleet and Agnes's tears, this was Charley's service.

Rangel put his arm around as much of her shoulders as it could reach, then wandered down the slope looking at names, some familiar. On one marble slab, he read "Billy Rose." Across from it was a one-room temple with ugly stained glass. "Agnes," he called. "Charley's in good company."

She looked through the sleet at the little man pointing to the sarcophagus.

"It's Gershwin. Wouldn't you know? Even here, we suck hind tit."

"Make sense, Charley."

Back in the limousine, Rangel looked at the sleet changing to drizzle and fog. The countryside was muffled in rat fur, the Hudson invisible. Rangel tried to think of

Double Charley

Charley, the amputation of Double Charley. He took Agnes's hand. "Maybe you should have let Olive see him."

"What?"

"She was just a security blanket. I know that. Still, a sad dumbie. Let her go up to the cemetery."

Agnes removed her hand.

"You were the only woman who ever counted for him."

"Hah."

"You were. The only one that understood him, that he could talk with."

"A lot you know, Charley."

"I knew him forty years, Agnes. No one but you better."

"No one knew the big stiff. Everyone knew parts of him."

"It's always like that. But we knew him most and loved him most."

"That's the truth."

"I wish he could have seen that dumb broad. She must have been something for him. At least, it was the last favor he could give anyone."

Agnes, florid, haughty, looked down at him. "That's what it would have been. The great favor-giver. The charm-distributor. That's where his career went. Everybody got his lyrics but you, Charley."

"I got enough. But Olive could have used one more."

Agnes picked at her heavy hair. (Charley moved away. Its odor was poor.) "She had no more business there than . . . Maggie."

"Sure she did. She was Charley's. For better or worse."

"And wasn't Maggie? Didn't she head out with him too? That was no great secret in New York. Why shouldn't she and sixteen others have been in the hospital room? He'd've found hands for them all. Oh God." Past and imagined wrongs clotted with her new solitude into a terrible bolus of feeling.

While she sobbed, Charley Rangel, arms out to hold what he could of her, felt his own head cracking. So that was the story. The stinking small grain of this world.

At 96th Street, the chauffeur made the fat turn off the Drive. Here in New York, Double Charley's last song began, the mean act of betrayal that was Charley Rangel's to set, to live with. "I'da punched his goddamn nose for him," he said. "I'd've bloodied the big bastard's nose."

Riordan's Fiftieth

Riordan's fiftieth birthday. For three years, it had been waiting for him; and here it was, a day like another, up before everyone, a cup of Instant, a corn muffin with marmalade, the six-block walk to Stony Island, the ride to the bus shed. He said nothing about it; but every other minute, it was there. Lucky he didn't drive Big Bertha up a lamp post. And thank God he had Route 12, a bit of air, a bit of green. When Lou Flint was fifty, three years ago, his missus turned the apartment into a parade float,there was everything but Playboy bunnies, and, all over, paper banners with "Half a Century of Flint" on them. The old lady had come on with a cake in Flint's own shape—what a shape, not far off a normal cake. And half the boys from the shift were there, there must have been forty, plus wives, it looked like Randolph and State. What a racket, what presents, and they'd drunk till time to go to work, there must have been fifty collisions and a thousand road fights that day in Chicago.

That was the way to pack it up.

And here he was, George Riordan, fifty to the day, and on his way home he'd had not one greeting and didn't know if his own kids had been told, but knew if he got a greeting out of her, it would leak out of the side of her moon face and make him feel "Who're you, Riordan, that anyone in the world should care you've weighted the planet fifty years?" The twins, ten years of Riordan spunk, would think it no different from any other day. They wouldn't remember that even last year they were making crayon pictures of cakes and missiles for him. "Happy Birthday, Dads," and big kisses, and she'd stirred herself enough to come up with a store cake, and Bill had carried it in and Joey had cut it up for them. She had refused her piece, though had not refrained, when he was off on the route the next day, oh no, had put half the cake in her gut, and when he'd asked for a piece that night, she said it had gone bad, they made it with month-old eggs, she wouldn't buy any more A & P cakes you bet your life, and, anyway, wasn't he a little long in the tooth to be stuffing himself with chocolate night after night, a coronary would clout him on the route, he'd kill a busload if not himself and be hauled off for prosecution in the courts, he'd damn better watch his weight, he wouldn't be able to stuff himself back of the wheel. This from Mrs. Fat herself.

Not a civil word to him for a week, and then, in front of the kids, this mouthful of sewage if he bothered to answer would make him so wroth he'd haul off and fetch her a clop round the ears.

What had happened? Where had his tranquility, where had his life gone?

104

Riordan's Fiftieth

Was she right, had it been a mistake from the start? One of her wild remarks that rang true? Four kids late. Why hadn't she stopped? God knows she had stopped the last years, he never even looked at her now, not that that slop of rump could get a rise from a three-year-old bull. A slob and a badmouther, this was what came of her, and the poor kids, living under this terrible roof with her leaking acid over them every day of their lives. No wonder Stan and Susie got out quick as they could. As if any other man could have stood her as long as he had without falling into a bit of comfort and sympathy. He hadn't moved a finger that way. Day after day, twenty-three years watching the birds climb on the bus, every shape and color of woman, legs climbing the steps, the skirts over the knees, let alone those skirts, where, practically in his eye, were thighs and more. And he had nothing but smiles and didn't know where to turn, only looking in the rear mirror and trying to steer.

What was it all about?

If the Cubs were warm in the race, at least there was something to look for; and in winter the Bulls and the Hawks, in the fall the Bears. All these animal teams he'd invested his heart in.

Not enough.

The folks were dead on the highway ten years now, Sis moved off to Detroit, and now the kids, Stan in the army, sure to go on to the lousy war, and Sue downtown calling up once a month, unable to hold her rage for his not sending her to college, her mother's tongue lashing him, who had been so dear a little girl, never a pouter, always fetching and kissing. As if he were Rockefeller. And she wouldn't even try the night course at Loyola or Wright Junior. Beneath her. No, above her, she never brought home the gold stars, the nuns said she was a dreamer, wouldn't concentrate. What did she dream about? The Beatles and worse. How did they fit her for college, even if he'd had the wherewithal?

There was a spoilage in this family. Maybe it was him. That was her view, he had that clear, though God knows short of lying around with a can of Schlitz watching the game, what was his life of luxury? Who had he made pay? Stan and the twins liked the games just like he. Every summer he took them off in the car for two weeks, Colorado, Texas, Vermont, they'd seen the whole country, thirty-nine states they'd been in. And stayed in the best motels, it cost God knows what over the years; added up, it would have sent Susan to college, Stan too. But what were they to do, all those years, live like clams in the dark? You had to get out of the city. God knows he couldn't blame the blacks down in Woodlawn, Kenwood, Lawndale, penned into those streets summer and winter, year after year. He might bust out and club a few heads himself given that.

So here he was, fifty, Susan a stranger and Stan in the army because he wasn't in college, and it was a rotten war, not the way it was in Korea where if you weren't gung-ho you were daft, and if you froze to death in the hills at least you knew you were keeping the Chinks from running the Pacific, and he hadn't lost so much as a fingernail. Perhaps better off if he'd come back minus an arm. Worse men than he were pulling ten thousand a year toting up figures at desks or bossing their betters in bottling plants and the white oil drums down in Whiting. Ten and fifteen thousand, and here he was, twenty-three years behind the wheel and finally making eighty-four hundred with three weeks in the summer. Plus the dread half your time you'd be hit on the head for the fares. He'd been damn lucky there, held up only twice and never been touched, knock wood. Now the fare box was locked, and the signs were up the drivers had no money, but there were heads and lushes all over, they stumbled up the steps with their dollar bills, didn't know or couldn't read, and one of these days, out on Route 10 or 11, one of them might slice him up for his shoes and his cap.

Not even the boys in the pool knew of his birthday. No loner, he just didn't shoot off his face. And wasn't close to anyone now. Two years ago, he'd dropped out of the card game. Elly could have made a scene if they'd come to the house; he'd said she'd taken sick, he had to stay and watch her. So no one said "Happy Birthday" and "Keep it Flying, Georgie." They talked as they always did. It was the vote for Manager of the Year and they'd passed over Weaver. "He only won a hundred and thirteen games and cleaned up the Reds in five." This from Powers. And he'd thrown in, wasn't that the way it always was, they always passed over the ones who did their jobs with their mouths shut and picked some flash with the bankroll behind him. "Like Durocher," said Powers, who grew up behind Comiskey Park and hated the Cubs. "No," he said, "Durocher took an armful of bums and kept them contending five years. He's loud but no bum." No point knocking good men. Though God knows Durocher showboated and mouthed.

The best of the day was the half-mile walk from Stony. Not the neighborhood it had been when they'd moved eighteen years ago, and true, it got worse each year. But it wasn't as bad as Elly's complaints that he'd kept them here while the blacks took over, knocking everyone over the head, and she scared to walk to the A & P except in broad daylight and then with her heart in her mouth. Maybe, but at six, with the night coming on, it was quiet and out of the stench of downtown, the air was breathable when the wind was up, they were close to the Lake, what he'd've given for that as a boy, and there were a few trees. Walking, he rolled. Cramped on a bus seat eight hours a day didn't slim you, and he started low to the ground as it was.

The streets still, small lawns in front of the stone three-flats, and every now and then a little home, the sort they'd aimed at for years, and if there hadn't been Stan's teeth, the surprise of the twins and the summer trips, that would be what they'd be living in now. Which might have kept her happy. Enough anyway to let him walk home tonight to a cake and his kids singing Happy Birthday over the candles so he could know he hadn't spent fifty years for nothing at all. So he was visible to someone. After all, his job was decent, he serviced more people in one week than most people in fifty, people of every type and look, and he went all over the city of Chicago, every four months taking the worst of its air—Route 7, where you moved up State on a Wednesday at noon at a mile an hour, the fumes of the tail pipes making hell in your lungs. And for eighty-four hundred a year while hamburger was seventy-five a pound. Oh Lord, this was wasting his mind on complaint. Here was a nice October night, the leaves falling, quiet in the streets, the air decent enough, he had four fine kids, he'd lived fifty pretty fair years, why fill the head with such garbage? Fifty years old, and inside no difference, no pains, maybe stiff in the back after the route, quicker to hit the sheets at night, but the same, and God knows if some decent woman, a widow like Mary Sears or a decent little cat-face spinster like Helen Whatshername—how long since he'd seen her, Easter Sunday at Holy Name—would say, "What about it, Georgie?" who knows if he mightn't take up the stakes and start for fresh. A woman, a real woman with sympathy and a body for his loneliness, and no more gaff and meanness. This sniping life while the boys looked on and ran off to the television to get out of the way.

Bad thoughts, and at his corner, there was lead in his heart, his key was lead, and his legs, and up the stairs past the college kids and the widow, and then, ah well, his own door, scratched, the pattern of scratches as close to him as his signature, and the noise of *McHale's Navy* from the machine and the slab of light from it as he passed to hang up his jacket, and her kitchen noise. "Good evening, Elly," he called toward it, and maybe there was a "Good evening" back at him and maybe not, and into the living room with Joey and Bill in the armchairs, and his hands on their heads. "Hello boys, how goes it today?" and got his "Hi Dads" from Bill, the plugger, and a colder "Hi" from Joey, Elly's product, who rose to affection only when food was in his mouth. Though he loved them both equally, they were dear boys, he couldn't take offense at Joey's coldness, the boy didn't know what he did or why, and now and then, out of the blue, the boy would pop up and kiss his cheek. They were good boys, he hoped he could get them into a decent trade, or, who knows, maybe college. If the present crop of wild ones didn't burn them all down by then. What a world.

Washing up, his face looked strange. The eyes seemed loose in the sockets, and his face thinner, maybe it was the new fluorescent which trimmed it down. A pug's nose, a chin like a boat keel, and what was left of his hair a rubble color, ash and brown. No face for the movies. Just George Riordan on his fiftieth. His own birthday cake.

Too late for the tv news, he lay on his bed and listened to

WGN. The usual garbage. They'd caught a hippie nut who'd killed a whole family out in the redwood country of California. The nuts of the world were everywhere. You were as safe in the middle of Chicago as anywhere. Nixon mouthed some guff to the United Nations, so fast you could hardly follow, if he wanted to speak why sound as if he didn't, the man was a phony, and this Agnew a showboat and mean to boot. And the wars, Arabs and Jews, and forty boys dead in Vietnam, and this the lowest count in years. But if one were Stan. Hundreds wounded, and they didn't tell you if it was sprained ankles, lost legs or worse. Maybe Stan would call. Last year he'd come home late, but in the morning he'd had a funny card from him. Signed "From a fellow fan." There'd be no chance Sue would call. She would remember and make a point of *not* calling. Or she'd call tomorrow and not say a word. Elly had handed her tongue on to Susan. Poor thing, poor girl making life miserable for herself. Selling shoes was a decent job for a girl without training, why wail you'd been given the short end of the stick? Seventeen, she had years to look around and try other things. Her mother's daughter, and God help the man who fell for her apple head, though God knows he still loved her and wouldn't want her to spend her life alone selling shoes. Why was she such a weight on him tonight? What had he done to turn her from him? Was it only college she'd wanted?

In the morning, he'd climb in the bus, and Harry would give him the finger and he'd come out of the pen, the great swiveling bus, and there would be that release, the roar and out in the morning. That's how the bus is. Years of it don't add up enough *to send you down to Loyola, and you didn't have the grades, my girl, for the nuns to set you up. What is it you want from me, darling? I wish I could give it to you yet.*

110

"Supper. Wash your hands, boys. Let's go."

The call that used to cheer his heart. He'd come into the roast after his day, the table set and the kids, four or two, and there'd be talk over the meat, and they'd pass round the chunks of potato and scoop out the beans, there'd be gravy for the beef and Brown Betty or ice cream for dessert, and coffee, ten or twelve colors on the table, and noise, and sometimes Sis and her husband, and sometimes no children only friends, and, years before, Mother and Dad.

And now what was there for the twins but a house of gloom. No one came, and even Stan and Susan were gone. Elly would not have his friends, saw only her pal the Mouth during the day. What idea of life would Bill and Joey have? That it was a tunnel of gloom, best out of it quickly. With dinner a call to a graveyard of feeling, to argument or silence, the only noise that of plates or Pass This or Mind Your Manners.

Tonight at least there was noise.

Joey said Bill hadn't washed, Bill said, "You're a liar," and he'd come in with, "I'll take a look, and don't let me hear such stuff in your mouth, you're brothers," and Joey said, "You're husband to mother, why do you fight?" and after a breath he got out with, "Older people have their differences over the years, and we're not the same flesh and blood, let alone twins, and keep respect in your mouth or I'll slap it there," and Elly said, "Let's forget talk of slapping, the both of you wash up your hands, you too, Joey, I can see the muck on them from here, and she sat down and put a breast of fried chicken on her plate and handed the platter down to him without a word.

"How's it go?" he tried.

"It went" she said. "You want to break down and try the peas?"

111

On his birthday she cooked the one vegetable he hated. "I haven't eaten a pea in twenty-five years."

"It might be the making of you." Bare arms, red, chafed, and the moon head with a tent of brown fluff, some sight for a man, yet her skin was clear and the green eyes. Years ago, years ago it had been a face. Now bunched with anger, the nose, mouth and chin crowding the middle. What waste.

The boys were back, Joey scowling. He asked them how school went.

"Same," said Bill. "Joey got throwed, oh well, never mind."

"Where did Joey get throwed?" from Elly.

"You mousefink. I'll get you, finko." Joey hot, and before the other mouthed back, he said, "I've had it from you two. One more little love song tonight, and I'll haul off and clap you for good."

A grumble from Joey with "You and who else" somewhere inside, but he took it as grumble. God knows he didn't want to break heads on this of all days.

"You can imagine where he finds his words," said Elly. "He don't need to read up in the dictionary. You might check your own mouth once in a while."

"Come on, Mom," said Bill, "Let's try it in peace." His plugging boy, a peacemaker at ten. Joey was into his chicken leg, grease over his face, lost. As if in a different part of the universe. Oh life was a raw, strange thing.

"It's not me wants war," she said, and held up a forkful of peas in toast to him. The actress. A hundred and eighty pounds of ham.

He put his fork on the plate with a noise, lifted his fists to the table, felt the silence, and said, "Boys, you know what?"

"What?" said Bill. Joey stopped jawing the leg.

"Your dad's at a milestone today."

He could feel thunder down the table, could feel her darken, feel the resentment, he was putting one over her, she who should have been springing surprise for him. But that wasn't what he wanted. He didn't want that.

Said Bill, "What's a milestone?"

"A milestone. It's something that's important. You know on the turnpikes, they have the signs giving you the mileage every mile. They used to be on white stones. Well, I'm at a big white stone today, I thought you'd like to know."

"You been fired, Dad?" said Joey, scared, the chicken leg shaking in his fist.

"No. I'm fifty years old today. It's my birthday, and a big one, and I'm going to take everyone over to Thirty-One Flavors for dessert, and you can have three scoops or four, whatever you want."

"Yay, Dads," said Joey, and out of his chair with the chicken leg and kissed his cheek.

And Bill came up, and said, "Happy Birthday, Dads. Wish I knowed, I'd made you a card," and kissed the other cheek.

And from her, "It slipped my mind. I thought it was next Friday. I had a cake on the list for it. Well here's looking at you," and she hoisted her coffee. It was something anyway. At least, for a minute. "And may the next fifty see you try harder."

"Thanks, Elly. The first fifty's the toughest."

"On who?"

There was no stopping her. It was like a child in her. Maybe the change of life would ease her. Let it pass tonight. What counted were these two, throwing them a

113

lifeline, giving them a boost. Too late for her. Maybe for him.

She didn't go with them, but till they went, there were no more slams, and the boys didn't fight, they felt something, and it was good to get out in the dark, the day had counted for something. Back in the car, he told the boys of Mother and Dad and how they'd come so close to seeing them born and how loved they'd have been and when they got back, Elly said, "Stan called to wish you returns of the day, he says he's fine," and there was a Hawks' game at eight from Maple Leaf Gardens, and Hull got the hat trick, first in the year. It was enough, more than he'd expected.

The moral was keep looking and waiting and maybe push it a little here or there, there's enough somewhere to celebrate, and maybe she was right, God knows, he could push harder the next fifty.

The Girl Who Loves
Schubert

Yntema and Scharf didn't like each other, but whenever Scharf came to New York—about once a year—they had lunch. Scharf would have finished his business and seen his few real friends, there'd be an open lunch date, why not call Yntema? They'd known each other thirty years, fellow law students at Ann Arbor, till Yntema dropped out, months shy of the degree.

During school, Yntema had gone with a girl, Marjory Spack, who was, he said, "Not my type. Beagle eyes and bandy legs." He introduced her to Scharf (who married her). A week after the introduction, Yntema took off for New York, found work in the Trust Department of the Chemical Bank and prospered.

Scharf was orderly, finicky, conservative; Yntema, erratic, flighty, a lover of disorder. When Yntema asked Scharf what was new, the answer would be something like, "I live like a plant. How different can leaves feel?" That was enough for Yntema. They could get down to his troubles, which were always rich; perfect matter for his fluent, seductive narratives.

Scharf adored them. (They compensated for his dislike of their hero.) Familiar as he was with their themes and tropes, there was always fine new detail. The themes were Yntema's father and his "endless declension of tarts"; Yntema's doubts of his masculinity, traceable, of course, to the paternal freebooter; Yntema's wives, girlfriends and therapies (sun cults, Tarot packs, LSD, jogging, diets), sources of his latest burst of "inner peace."

Almost every year there was a new wife or friend. "How's Felicia?" On his one visit to Yntema's West End Avenue apartment, Scharf had had a glimpse of her.

"I'm sure she's getting along. Why?"

"So there's a new installation."

"I'm with a terrific girl. A brilliant, tough girl. I met her at the Midtown Club. Weight-lifting. I started lifting in May."

"You're looking very solid."

"Three times a week at the Club. And at home; with Walter." Walter was Yntema's eighteen-year-old son. "It's quite a sight, the two of us grunting under iron."

Walter's moods, schools, clothes, analysts and drug bouts were a subtheme of Yntema's saga. Walter was "an index to his generation," a sociological thermometer luckily found in Yntema's own medicine chest.

Yntema had an abnormally quiet but lyric voice. Its lilt was that of repression: repressed laughs, repressed boasts, repressed feelings of every sort. Marjory Scharf remembered it as "a fake seducer's voice. A meadow disguised as a minefield." Laughter was always swelling in it. Then something held it back, and out came snorts and melancholy honks.

Scharf, who'd run to fat and was gray at forty, marveled at Yntema's looks. For all the divorces, the self-doubts, the expressed and suppressed hatreds, Yntema looked much the same as he had at Ann Arbor. Fifty-one, there were scarcely any lines in his face; no gray hair, just less black, less curl above a face that looked like a mix of Byron and Pushkin.

Over tea and *sushi,* Yntema said that Felicia's successor, Apple Gruber, was "the girl who loves Schubert. Remember *A Handful of Dust?* The fellow trapped in the jungle by that lunatic illiterate who makes him read Dickens's novels aloud over and over? That's me. Except I only have to listen, and Apple's unfortunately literate. She has this dowser's gift of knowing what I don't. 'Have you read this, have you read that?' 'No.' So it's lecture time. I might as well be back in Ann Arbor with all that rigged knowledge. You know how these Sardinian kidnappers always ask for just the amount of dough the guy's got in the bank. They're in cahoots with the bankers. Who's in cahoots with Apple?"

"You must give yourself away."

"The inner banker. May be. She gets intellectual crushes. Last spring it was Leibniz. Our place turned into an Institute. Ferney West. Optics; hydrostatics; pneumatics; mechanics; calculus. There was nothing the old kraut wasn't into. *La vraie logique, l'art de calculer, l'art d'inventer.* Monads crawling around. Four months of Leibniz. Until ten o'clock, November 27. We're at Lincoln Center listening to Fischer-Dieskau singing Schubert. And boom, zoom,

117

out the room. That night, the monads get the sack. Boole, Frege, Russell, Peano, all those great Leibnizian logicians who'd battered my head since August, are out. November 29 I come home from work and halfway up the elevator I hear Fischer-Dieskau singing *Die Winterreise.*" And Yntema sang, "*'Manche Trän aus meinen Augen.'* On every chair, scores; albums; articles; biographies. Apple, who's a terrific Amazon—you should see her, she's spectacular, it's like making love to the Brooklyn Bridge—she's—what?— swathed, enshrouded in a cloud of tulle. A golden peignoir. My Viennese Alp. Muscles? They're out too. Hair—which had been tied up in a nice lump—is a blizzard. A red blizzard, halfway to Egypt. On the walls are watercolors, lithographs, woodcuts. The Vienna woods, the Danube, the Prater, Metternich, Beethoven. A week later, Schubert himself shows up. In bronze. Eyeglasses and all. Six hundred bucks."

"On you?"

"Are you nuts?"

"What does she do?"

"Physical therapy for retarded kids. Riding and rowing. Rich she is not. But what there is goes to Vienna. I live in a Schubert Museum."

If anything, Yntema's apartment looked like a museum of Radical Nostalgia. Yntema lived his idea of the thirties intellectual, domiciled, but ready to go underground at the first knock. His building's tiny lobby had a defunct carpet, puce walls, an ancient elevator, dark corridors. Varnish scabs ribbed the doors. Yntema's apartment was the natural bloom of this shabbiness. Its walls were the same yellow-puce as the lobby's—there must have been a paint sale around the corner—the chairs and the sofa had long since had it. When you rose from them, clumps of hair rose

118

with you. As for décor, Scharf remembered a swatch of frayed batik tacked between an unframed map of Europe and a Woolworth-framed lithograph of the British Museum Reading Room. The room stank of pamphlets.

Why did Yntema live like this? Alimony, doctors, girls and Walter were expensive, but he made lots of money. If ever a place staged an idea, it was this one. The idea was, "The hero of a mental saga needs no scenery."

Yntema was living with Felicia Mellowine, a very long-necked redhead he'd "rescued from the turpitude of Gimbel's. Decorative Accessories. Eight hours a day, no sitting down or leaning on counters. Eighty-five dollars a week." Scharf saw Felicia for about a minute and a half. (Though quite a lot of her, for she wore nothing but a blue dressing gown that had served some of Yntema's more careless companions. He tried not to stare at the navel and nipples which winked through the holes.)

"Who's Lawrence of Arabia?" The voice didn't do justice to the beautiful throat.

"Why?" asked Yntema. He did not look up from his can of Blatz.

"Kojak asked this cop who he thought he was, 'Lawrence of Arabia?'"

"President of OPEC," said Yntema.

"An Arab?" Above the neck, Felicia was mostly pout.

"Say hello to Ed Scharf, kiddo."

"Hi Ed. I won't bother you. I'm into a good show."

Were all Yntema's women—after Marjory, of course— such washouts? They were so vivid in his stories. Perhaps what counted for him was not the girl but what he could invent about her. The less there was to work with, the more he could invent.

119

Or was this *his* invention? Was he Yntemizing? Making his own Yntema saga?

After all, Yntema radiated intelligence and self-control. The quiet voice was sane and clear.

"A few weeks ago, Walter and I are lifting away, dripping, concentrating. You don't lift, there's a lot to it. The idea's to put every muscle against its pain wall, then drive through it. You have to concentrate every second. Otherwise you'll break. So we're lifting, and all of a sudden I feel something. A glance. A shaft. I've got a hundred and seventy pounds in the air, and I spot the *schöne Müllerin* leaning delicately on the wall. Looking. 'Do you boys know what you're doing?' Remember, this girl has *thighs, biceps,* she bench-presses a hundred and forty pounds. 'Is this what you really want? I mean, what's the *point?* Walter'— Walter's stretched out, he looks like a weather map— 'Walter,' she says, 'do you know that when Schubert was eighteen he composed two symphonies, three sonatas and a hundred and forty-five songs? Does that give you pause, Walter?' Walter's so proud of these muscles, Eddie. You know he's not a big guy, eczema's crawling over him, what does the kid have but these muscles? He's worked like a dog for them. I mean what does Walter have to do with some one-in-a-trillion phenomenon who sneezed music? Push Schubert downstairs, the stairs sang.

"So that's life *bei* Yntema. Not all bad. I like to learn. And the first ten times you hear the *Winterreise,* it's everything Apple says it is. But that's the thing about this girl. She doesn't have the usual appetite. No one who looks like Babe Diedrickson—plus Maureen O'Hara—can have a normal appetite. She can't stop with anything. And with Schubert, it's not the songs she wants, it's what they

The Girl Who Loves Schubert

conceal. What they mean. We had to hear this *Winterreise* till she figured out how it killed Schubert."

"I don't get that."

"It's baloney. That is, sure Apple. Her Schubert had a terrific life. His family loved him, he had great friends, they had these wine-drinking parties where he sang his songs. He composed every day, studied scores, read poems. He was smart as hell, read everything, classics, Goethe, Fenimore Cooper, discovered Heine. And he knew he was great stuff. Then he read these *Winterreise* poems; full of drivel about a guy wandering around the snow, a kind of *lumpen* Lear, barked at by dogs and so on. He goes crackers and ends up with an organ-grinder. Apple's idea is Schubert took every word of this drivel and turned it on himself: he had no one, no girl, no real friend, nobody to understand what he was about. Except Beethoven, who'd just died. Schubert went to the funeral, and that set him up for his own."

"He killed himself?"

"*Typhus abdominalis.* Same thing his mother died of. But Doktor Gruber, Professor of Viennese *Schwärmerei*, says it's 'essentially suicide. The virus sits around waiting till it gets a mental cue.' Then boom, zoom, out the room."

Within Yntema's stories, there were always others. His saga was not a mere odyssey of bruises. Every bruise meant something. Schubert meant something. Apple meant something. The real story was always Yntema's, and Scharf knew that he discovered it as he told the other. That was why Yntema relished their lunches.

"Are you waiting for Schubert to go the way of Leibniz? Is that where you stand?"

Yntema tongued some *saki*, very thoughtfully. "Don't

you see?" Oystery light from the perforated brass shades touched his eyes, teeth, cheekbones. He was like a little festival of insight.

Yntema had his narrative tricks: he held back, called for the check, went through the rigmarole with credit card, receipt, signing, tip, and it was ten minutes—while they walked up 46th Street in their topcoats—before Scharf pushed him toward the end of the installment. "I don't see what you think *she* was getting at."

"I don't either. Yet." Yntema stopped. They were in front of the bank. "At first I thought, 'She's trying to get rid of Walter.' But she likes him. If only as another listener. It's something else.

"Leibniz was a force for her, a mentality, not a person. Schubert's something else; a presence. A person. One she takes to. His fecundity, his modesty, his confidence, even his smallness—he was four-eleven!—reproach her. And enchant her. What does that make me? Superfluous. Three's a crowd. The question is, 'Is she *gunning* for me?' Not with a gun. An Apple doesn't do it with a gun. The gun she uses is *you.*"

"Me?"

"Me! She uses you against yourself. Like Walter's muscles. *Die Winterreise.* She's contriving a *Winterreise* for me. An internal boot in the ass. And out goes Yntema. Into the snow."

The sun blinds the glass skins of Sixth Avenue. "The U. S. of A., Eddie. Shining, stretching, pushing, remaking. 'Oh say, can you see?' No? 'Then move on. The frontier. Build the sonofabitch over. The Indians? Grind'm.' Apple—Christ! her name's Martha!—she's pure American. Apple pie. And I've eaten of the apple. I've gotta pay. So that's where it stands. Am I Apple's eye? Or her Indians?"

The Girl Who Loves Schubert

*   *   *

The annual installment often ended like a serial, Yntema dangling over a sexual cliff. But Scharf was in on it; it existed because of him. As if Yntema had troubles in order to have a new installment for their lunches.

There was some ill-will here as well: if Yntema dangles, why not Scharf? Scharf knew that Yntema was more than puzzled by his steadiness. His self-deprecations—"I live like a plant"—"I'm a uxorious vine"—offended Yntema as patronizing superiority: "He can afford self-deprecation."

Scharf was happy. He loved not only his routines but the idea of them. That fact was beyond or beneath Yntema's comprehension. He resented such vegetal contentment as a worldly as well as a Scharfian fact. How could a human being who was neither prude nor dummy restrict himself in a world so rich with possibility? Scharf felt that Yntema must think he was lazy, or that his energy was low. A wife of thirty years must be a security blanket, a form of avarice or fear. "And maybe that's right," Scharf conceded. Still, the concession didn't disturb him. The fact that he could imagine Yntema's views protected him from them. Which was his equivalent of Yntema's technique: surviving trouble by recounting it.

Scharf got back to New York a year from the next January and didn't call Yntema till his last day there. Yntema's secretary said he hadn't come to work.

"All these years I've known him, he's never missed a day," Scharf said, not quite to himself.

"I'm afraid he's missed quite a few lately."

It would have been the third time in a quarter of a century that they hadn't gotten together. But there was a blizzard in Chicago, no flights were going in. Scharf called

Yntema's home from LaGuardia. Any chance of their getting together, he'd tried him yesterday at the office.

"Why not?" said Yntema, thickly.

"You don't sound well, Sidney. Can I bring aspirin? Di-Gel?"

"Bring a few cold cuts. You know Zabar's."

The abruptness, plus the canceled flight, the changed venue of their get-together, and then the snow, which started coming down as he rode back into town, pushed Scharf toward depression. The ride was slow, the air heavy. Still, after checking back into the Westbury, he felt better. He taxied to Zabar's and hauled off twenty dollars' worth of corned beef, pastrami, Swiss cheese and Kaiser rolls.

Yntema's lobby sported a green-mold paint and, in place of the defunct carpet, a corrugated rubber runner. The elevator groaned worse than ever, the corridors were as grim, and the front door sicker of varnish than it was three years ago.

Yntema too was in bad shape. He limped, his eyes were dull, the black curls were stippled with gray, and his arms and shoulders seemed at odds with his T-shirt.

The living room was also the worse for wear. Neither map, lithograph, nor batik swatch festooned the puce walls. The room looked as if it had been in a fight. A leg of the coffee table was taped, there was a purple stain on the unhappy sofa.

Scharf followed limping Yntema into the kitchen— another piece of misery, though not a battleground. They unloaded the delicatessen onto poorly cleaned plates, and took cans of Blatz out of the only ice box with a spherical motor on top that Scharf had seen since World War II. "I've seen better days," said Yntema.

124

The Girl Who Loves Schubert

"I can see that." The room, Scharf realized, was bare of music. No scores, no albums, no bust of Schubert. "Apple taken up another subject?"

"Did she not, Eddie. Very bad scene here." Yntema's pitch was odd; and there was something askew in his face. "Not pleasant."

"Bit of a brawl?"

"Hell of a brawl. The bitch did for me. Christ, it's hard to manage these rolls." His teeth squirreled around the Kaiser roll.

Scharf looked closer. The fixity, the evenness, the whiteness of the teeth. Proud-mouthed Yntema had a denture. Still, he wolfed, pastrami bits falling on his jeans, the chair, through the slit in the Blatz can.

"I'm glad I stayed over. I wanted to hear how things were going."

To his surprise and pleasure, Yntema let out a considerable—unrepressed—laugh. "Hear? Look!" He spread arms, pastrami in his left hand, beercan in his right. *"Yntema Bound.* Act Five."

"She really gave it to you."

"Nose. Teeth. Concussion. She threw the goddamn bust at me. Which I'd tried to bust. If I'd have been two feet closer, she'd have killed me. What an arm. She got my ankle with the barbell. There's lots of Blatz." He hoisted his empty and Scharf brought him another, thinking, "There's no pleasure seeing him so low." Which surprised him.

Was it that he was actually *seeing*, not just hearing about it? It was just bruise, not storied bruise.

Story did come out; at least story-matter. Slowly, and with little verve. "Felicia started it."

"She came back?"

125

"Not to me. I saw her. On the street. Recognized her neck."

"Not *cut!*"

"Mink doesn't cut. And that little red nut of a head under more mink. Standing outside Armando's. You and I ate there, five or six years ago." Scharf nodded. "I called her. She turned, saw me, her mouth flew open and she got red as her hair. I thought she was going to pass out. I had no idea. Then I see the old bastard coming out of Armando's."

Yntema looked at Scharf, who picked it up. "Your father?"

"Dr. Tart-Eater himself. I don't know how she found him. Or he her. I don't want to know. But there he was holding on to the mink. He saw me, started to say something, I saw his mouth twisting for it, but she pulled him off. Five years ago, he'd have kicked her into the gutter. Now he's a thousand years old; he just got pulled off. What a moment. I leaned against the menu board. Asking myself, 'What does this say about my life? My choices? Am I just a continuation of that pig?'" Yntema's voice had more lilt in it now, and some dental clicks as well. "Every time I've thought, 'He can't go lower,' he does. 'Pitched past pitch of' *pitch*. And what about me? Where did he pitch me?"

Scharf pointed to the battered room, to Yntema's face, his ankle. "I still don't see the connection."

"I took off, just walked uptown. I got home. Apple was out rowing her kids in Central Park. There was this"— hoisting the salted curls toward what was no longer there—"Viennese *merde* all over. Spectral *merde*. Musical *merde*. Bronze *merde*. I was so low. I felt like I was being played, like a record. Then I just let rip. I hit Franz Peter with the barbell. Right in the eyeglasses. Bashed them into the nose. Knocked a chunk of it off. I flattened him, then flattened his albums. Crazy, just crazy. In my whole life, I never got a drop of beer on a library book. That afternoon I tore them up. Scores, articles, books. Terrible."

"You didn't knock your own teeth out."

"I needed help there. You're sitting on my blood. Or hers. What a battler. But I busted her too. She came home to the wreckage and went crazier than I. Threw her damn Schubert at my face. When I came to, the two of them were sitting on me. Then the Super came. Pacified her. They must've heard the racket on Broadway. A woman scorned is nothing. Smash a god, that's when you get fury. Imagine where I'd be if she'd been lifting weights all those months. As it was, I was two weeks in Lenox Hill. I just got off the crutches."

Scharf had to spend another day in New York—O'Hare was still closed—but there was no question of seeing Yntema again. He felt that he'd identified a body; the saga was over. Oh, Yntema was off crutches, there'd be a few more turns, more spills, another girl, and another, but what counted for Scharf was over. Ulysses had come home. To nothing worth singing about. (The only songs that survived here were Schubert's.)

That afternoon, Scharf, about to pass a record store, went in and bought the Fischer-Dieskau recording of the *Winterreise*. For some reason he didn't bother working out, it seemed the right coming-home present for Marjory.

A Recital for the Pope

1

In 1567, Carlo Lombardo built a palace for Prince Aldo
Lanciatore on the site of the Porticus Linucia which in 110
B.C. had been raised by the Consul M. Linucius for the
distribution of corn to the Roman plebs. In the late
seventeenth century, a master of less altruistic distribu-
tions, the papal banker Giorgio Fretch, bought the palace
from the Lanciatore family and summoned a pupil of
Borromini, Fulvio Praha, to remake the façade into one of
the aimlessly turbulent extravaganzas of Roman baroque.
For years now, tours of Roman palazzi, on route from the
Cancelleria to the Farnese, have stopped to heave a few
laughs at the combination zoo, arboretum, orchard, and

129

mythological wood which Praha's workmen churned from the warm yellow tufa rock and its protective stucco, but in the seventeenth century, this blast at vitruvian chastity excited the cupidity of numerous Roman families of whom the Quadrata were the most insistent. They purchased the Lanciatore and held it in their possession until the first World War erased their line.

A month after Mussolini was installed in the Palazzo Venezia, the Lanciatore was bought for a song and his Spanish whore by Elisha Borg of the Standard Oil Company of Indiana, who, converted by the woman, left it surprisingly, not to her, but to the Dominican Order, on condition that it be established as an institute where well-bred American Catholic girls could become yet more refined under the tutelage of the sisters and the amorous frescoes of Domenichino, Guercino, Albani, and Lanfranco.

Each June since 1951, eight American girls paid three thousand dollars apiece for a year's board and room, joined in artistic community by two somewhat older Spellman Scholarship Students, one of whom always came from Europe. In 1962, the American Spellman Scholar was a poet from Providence, Rhode Island, named Nina Callahan.

Nina knew Dominicans: her brother had joined the order at twenty, and, at twenty-one, had been able to let her in on the Dominican strategy of humbling the sharpies and exalting the occasional nulls who'd crept into the fold. The sharpies would find themselves peeling onions in Kansas kitchens while the nulls would be living it up in European palaces.

The four Palazzo Lanciatore nulls were Sister Clara, a withered thirty-year-old blonde who ran the kitchen ("into

130

the devil's throat" said Nina to her one friend among the girls, Sibyl Taylor); Sister Mary Pia, a terrier-faced woman, whose self-imposed duty was waiting up for the girls coming back from Rosati's and the Veneto hangouts with the local counts, princelings and other loafers, discouraging manifestations of affection and insinuating improprieties; Sister Louella, an immense, gentle lesbian whose pleasure it was to see that the girls never learned anything which would further liberate what she regarded as their inordinately free persons; and Sister Angie Caterina, a moronic dwarf assigned to the maintenance of the musical instruments and art supplies which the girls were supposedly utilizing in their direct encounters with the Roman muses.

The nulls were bad enough to sour Nina's first weeks in Rome, the girls and their luxurious idleness disturbed her slightly more, but what chiefly coiled her insides was the desecration of the real magnificence which had been accumulated behind Praha's façade in the four centuries of the Lanciatore's existence: the plastic Standa lampshades on the bronze Renaissance lamps, the dangling rips in the Licorne tapestry, the peeling Bassano landscape which sweated over an unsheathed radiator, the Lipton tea bags which daily sank in the chipped gold cups, the paperback detective stories which lined the cypress panels under the begrimed cherubs of the quattrocento cantoria, the ceiling's smoked lunettes, the crumbling egg-and-dye friezes, and the courtyard where weeds overran patterns and tumuli fattened in the lawn; a general squalor of ignorance such as Nina, in years of living from hand to mouth in cavelike rooms from Dublin to Vienna, had never encountered.

In her third week at the palace, Nina secured Sister

Clara's careless permission to draw on the bulging maintenance fund for supplies and repairs. Before the sisters woke
up to what was going on, she had summoned gardeners,
masons, plasterers, painters, carpenters, electricians, and a
piano tuner, ordered a thousand dollars' worth of books for
the library, another thousand dollars' worth of art supplies—there having been not a piece of armature wire or
canvas in the studio, which was used exclusively by the
girls' dressmakers—and spent two weeks supervising the
workmen and cruising the Via Babuino for a few indispen-
sable replacements.

At the very point of triumphant conversion, the sisters'
dull awareness was, not shocked, but penetrated by the
reparatory swirl. Recoiling from the signs of sodomic
luxury, they traced them to Nina and confronted her en
bloc to tell her that she should let them attend to "the
housework" so that she could take full advantage of her
unique opportunity to live in splendor.

Shaken to tears, Nina could think of nothing to say but
that in Francis L. Callahan's house one never found a
paper napkin by one's plate nor month-old stains on the
tablecloth. Though even this was not said aloud. Nina had
no use for fruitless rebellion. The one response in her stay
at the Lanciatore which even hinted disrespect followed
one of Sister Louella's rebukes that she was not paying
attention to the news broadcasts which gashed their every
dinner hour in the interest of "keeping up" both Italian
and knowledge of the world: "Sister, my mind is not good
enough for current events."

Nina was a pixie of a woman, small, finely built, cup-
jawed, flat-nosed, merry-faced; only blue eyes showed the
ire which followed such trampling on her passion for
rectitude and beauty. Had it not been for one thing, she

might have headed back to Paris then and there. But the one thing was a great temptation.

Each September, after the Pope's return from Castel Gandolfo, he received the girls of the Palazzo Lanciatore in private audience. Indeed, each girl was alone with the Pope for three minutes, and then joined the others for a group photograph. Framed in Standa's rhinestoned squares, the papal photographs lined the central hallway into the music room.

Nina craved those three minutes. She admired, even loved the round little pope, discerned a translucence in his peasant's vulpine face which marked a sympathy of the highest order. He was clearly someone who responded to the finest human notes, perhaps as much or even more than his elegant predecessor, Pacelli (another favorite of Nina's). She could endure eight weeks of the nulls for this.

As if to mark the time, she undertook another reclamation project, that of the chief human rent in the Lanciatore. This was the year's European Spellman Scholar, Červa Grbisz, who'd come from Cracow with a cardboard valise to pursue her violin studies at the Conservatory. Červa's valise contained neither toothbrush, comb, nor bar of soap. Červa was fetid. Her hair was a knot of greasy filth, her teeth a gangrenous yellow, her breath a reek of garbage. She owned two dresses; both bore sweat marks, armpit to hip, bloody purple on the dark dress, grainy chestnut on the light. When she entered a room, occupants gulped, swallowed, took off. It was this which began to perturb Červa enough to consult her fellow Spellman Scholar. Why was it, she asked, that others did not take to her? Didn't Americans like foreigners? After all, she was a Spellman Scholar, chosen for her adaptability as well as her mastery of English.

133

Nina made a quick, a "Catholic," decision. Yes, she told Červa, she was sure the girls would take to her in time, they were slow to make friends with people overseas, and by the way, wasn't Roman heat terrible on one's hair. "I used to have to wash mine every single night." She took up a bottle of Dop. "Except I found this stuff in Prima. You only have to wash every other day with it. You take this one. I've got another bottle."

"I don't have no hair trouble," said Červa.

"Try it anyway, I'll bet you'll have the same luck I did."

"Your hair don't appear different to me."

Nina did not give up. With Elizabeth Arden soapcakes, Pepsodent toothpaste—"A new American product, worked out in a laboratory for Roman women"—cologne water, eyebrow tweezers, nail files, combs—"specially designed for the Roman summer"—and then with the dresses, skirts, blouses and cardigans which the girls actually tossed into wastepaper baskets after dressmaking and shopping sessions, Nina tried, but although Červa relaxed once or twice into taking something, it was only to appease Nina, for neither her skin, hair, teeth, nor wardrobe were exposed to the menaces which so ruffled the little American.

Červa cared for only two things, the Church and her music. She could barely contain her joy in the forthcoming audience. As for the music, she treated the girls to a sample of it during an afternoon tea while Sister Clara lunged accompaniment at one of the Lanciatore's newly tuned Steinways. Face lit with religious and musical fervor, Červa ground a Tartini sonata into such excruciation that only Nina and Sibyl survived *in situ;* and Nina survived only by resolving to end her futile attempts to gild the weed. It was high time to return full time to her own work.

Nina's work, the core of her life, was the realization of a

plan she'd mapped out when she was sixteen. The plan was to become a major poet. This meant a profound study of the poetic accomplishment of the race. In eleven years, three in the United States, the rest in Europe, Nina filled almost all time not spent earning dinner and rent money tracking the great achievements of poetry in the eight languages she studied. In New York, Chicago, San Francisco, London, Dublin, Madrid, Paris, Berlin, Vienna and then Paris again for the last two years, Nina scrounged for the eight or nine hundred dollars a year she needed to live by guiding, nursing and accompanying tourists, waiting on tables, drawing caricatures, playing piano in bars, clerking, helping in art galleries, begging, borrowing, and when really necessary, stealing. Waking without knowing where the day's meal would come from, far from dismaying, cheered and stimulated her. She thought of herself as a citizen of time, not space. Her country was Poetry.

The Spellman Scholarship was another of the things into which Nina fell. Her Dominican brother had sent her name and book of poems into the selection committee. Although she was the only applicant who had so exposed herself to the public, it was decided to take a chance on her. Nina had qualms about leaving Paris, but was talked into thinking the award a sign of special grace and came with an eagerness that only the nuns dimmed.

In mid-July, she went back on the schedule she'd mapped out eleven years before, mornings in the library, afternoons seeing things, evenings writing. The schedule was pleasant habit, not constraint. Nina never hesitated to alter it for friends, concerts, or laziness. After breakfast at the Lanciatore, she walked as fast as the rising heat allowed across the Tiber to the Vatican Library where she stayed till it closed at one. She was working on a plutarchan comparison between the poets of the Greek Anthology and the early Italian poets from Ciullo d'Alcamo to the *dolce stil nuovo,* using the *Volgari Eloquentia* as a guide. Her interest was in patterns of cadence, syntax, meter, diction, pitch, stress, junctions (she had also studied linguistics on her own), and the relationship of forms to topics. She did research into musical settings, one of her ambitions being to revive the *sagen-und-singen* techniques of the *Minne* and Provençal poets. It was exciting work. Leaving the library was as difficult as anything that preceded or followed it. She walked back along the rattling avenues to where her free lunch sat engulfed by Červa, the sisters, and the two or three girls who'd stood up their midday dates. Then, without siesta, she trolleyed around the city by the *circolare,* getting off at handsome prospects, museums and churches.

Rome wasn't, however, exciting her as she'd imagined it would. There were wonderful things at the Villa Giulia and the Diocletian Museum, there were fine views and churches, but more and more the transistors and Vespas which blasted her ears combined with the punitive sun to give her massive headaches. Then, too, the imperial assertions of the embassies, the Bernini squares and Bernini fountains depressed Nina: like the aimless contortions of baroque churches, they proclaimed their egomania. It was as if the sisters had governed Rome since Bramante's time.

At night, dinner behind her, Nina's life came into focus. Looking over the Campo dei Fiori, the odors of the day's market still afloat, Nina's mind sought the precise articulation of thought, feeling, memory. In the dark solitude, old accomplishment married novel expression. Not even Červa's violin wrestling devils across the hall ruined her meditations.

A Recital for the Pope

In late July, Nina found herself involved with Sibyl
Taylor's problems. Sibyl too was discontented with the
Lanciatore. She trailed along with Nina, buying beautiful
piles of fruit and ice cream, discoursing on her problems
with amorous Romans. Sibyl was extremely pretty, blond,
pleasant, sensitive. Nina, who liked gossip as well as
anyone, found her a great relief from the whistlers and
pinchers who were the only people with whom she had any
words at all when she went round the city by herself.

Sibyl's most recent problem was not with a Roman but
an American named Edward Gunther who'd come up to
her in San Pietro in Vincoli to explain Freud's theory
about the Moses statue. This had led to an aperitif and
talk, hours of talk. Surprisingly, Edward had forgotten to
take her address, but the next Sunday, he'd shown up at
San Clemente, the church to which the sisters took them
every Sunday because it was run by Irish Dominicans.
Sibyl noticed him when he'd snorted at Sister Louella
lifting Sister Angie Caterina like a poodle into and out of
her seat. Sister Clara had pinned him with a fierce look.

Edward was large, black-haired, soft-looking, lively.
He'd been in Rome a month longer than Sibyl and Nina,
had neither job, function nor plan. "I'm relaxing a sick
heart," he said, but did not invite questions about it. Nina
felt some sort of truth in that, but also felt it was a
smokescreen. For what, she didn't know. In any event,
Edward was a continuous instructor about things Roman.
Instructing, his face flamed with eagerness, his gestures
with illustrative fluidity. Nina interpreted all this fire and
liquidity as more than pedagogy. She also realized that it
was not meant only for Sibyl. That did not worry *her*. She'd
handled far subtler propositioners.

One staggeringly hot day, they drove out to Hadrian's
Villa in Edward's Fiat Cinquecento. "Small but the

motor's air-cooled." They weren't. Amidst the ruins, they sweltered and Edward lectured. Quite brilliantly. He'd read up on the Villa and knew where in the white rubble everything had been, theater, atrium, the model of Tartarus.

After an hour, the sun mastered the master. Edward led them to a dead pool where filthy ducks cruised sullenly over the scum. He and Sybil removed their shoes, put their feet through the disgusting veneer and rubbed them against each other's. Nina felt more superfluous than the ducks. She wandered off while Edward, renewed by Sybil's feet, was engaged in a comparison of Hadrian with "those broken-down artists who become dictators, Napoleon and Mussolini—ninth-rate novelists—Hitler, a tenth-rate painter." She found a piece of shade under an umbrella pine. Heat-misted miles away, lay Rome. *Animula, blandula, vagula:* Hadrian's poem to his little jokester-companion. Jokester-companion. That was like her own rôle here. Those clumsy, at-the-brink lovers, playing footsie in the scum. Or were they clumsy? How would she know? Scholar-priest of Amor, she had heard the subtlest confessions of those apt in its words, Ovid, Gottfried, Ciullo, Cavalcanti. *Ailas. Tant cujava saber/D'amor, et tant petit en sai:* To know so much *about* love and know *it* so little. Nothing that she'd read had matched what she'd felt in the occasional Irish arms which held her in automobiles, on dance floors outside the half-mile limit of Francis L. Callahan's honorable home on Water Street. Not that she was a Louella, not that she had hormonic deficiencies, though, worried, she had gone to a doctor at sixteen and gotten a shot of estrogen to see if it would ease her ability to be gratified by the local pawers. It hadn't. There was always something askew, a psychological oxymoron, a gulf between desire and perception. Her body, shaped for

138

passion, if she could believe the Providence locals and transient hot shots from Dublin to Vienna (or, for that matter, the mirror) had felt nothing more than an odd, erratic itch which, she knew, must never become necessity. No Edwards need apply. She had what she had, far more than scum-rubbing with a professional mouther. What was she doing here anyway? Here in the ruined villa? Here in Rome? Free grub three times a day? Not enough. She'd survived years without institutional handouts. Kroening, the nutty Swede, who'd corresponded with Tolstoi, had given her a cottage in Brittany; Hauch, the Berlin painter, shared his room and food despite her refusal to share herself; Mrs. Mackie had supported her in Dublin on her Guggenheim and taught her Celtic to boot. Best of all, Mademoiselle, whom she'd deserted, yes it amounted to that, to come here, her neighbor for two years in the attic on Rue de l'Université. Mademoiselle Laguerre. Minute, aged, horribly poor, yet so graceful amidst the propped wreckage, drunks and shriekers of that attic, she was like a Benedictine among the vandals. The ideal citizen, articulate, curious, the happy frequenter of museums and libraries, the thoughtful reader of discarded newspapers, a preserver of all that was handsomest in her marginal past: the two eighteenth century Limoges cups in which she served tea (cracks away from her guest), the lace gloves, one soiled (and so always carried in the other), the thirty books, read almost to dust. A purer version of Francis L., really, a man whom Nina had never seen in shirtsleeves, who governed six children by eyebrow and finger motion, by a high unmentioned honor which could have sustained her through two lifetimes of passionate temptations. Mademoiselle and Nina spent fifty hours a month talking, about Indo-China, books, Debussy.

Three months before Nina left for Rome, Mademoiselle

139

showed her an inventory of her possessions, cups, gloves, books. By each item was the name of the intended recipient, *"en cas d'une éventualité."* Nina was to get the books, the clothes were to go to the old lady who came upstairs twice a week for the doilies, her money—about sixty thousand old francs—was to go with her fan, a few daguerrotypes, and the cups to a distant niece. With the inventory was a receipt for a cemetery plot and funeral service in the 18th arrondissement. Nina took the papers and no more was said. A few days later, Nina came to Mademoiselle with news of the Spellman award. *"Oh, ma chère,"* said Mademoiselle, "I needed no confirmation of your powers, but I am thrilled. It is a sign of special favor."

Nina didn't want to leave. "They don't include the fare to Rome, Mademoiselle." Mademoiselle took fifty thousand francs from a drawer. "I feel so lucky to be able to do this, Nina."

Nina would have gone if only to accept the money. Now, under the umbrella pine, she felt the departure as desertion, and worse, desertion into the falsity, show and noise which art and Mademoiselle's life fought to the death. She'd go back, if she had to sell Červa's violin. She'd go back after the papal audience.

2

The Lanciatore steamed with preparations. Sister Angie Caterina's muttering swelled with the excitement she barely understood. Sister Clara attacked swatches of black poplin so that Červa would make a suitable appearance. The girls stunned their dressmakers with demands for spectacular simplicity. Each three minutes with the Pope was to be an indelible picture for him.

A Recital for the Pope

On the great day, four taxis deposited sisters and students in front of the Vatican apartments. They walked up marble flights, passed glittering salons, the girls ogled the piked Switzers, were themselves ogled by papal secretaries. Then they were ushered into an antechamber whose golden magnificence staggered even these young productions of Grosse Point and Winnetka.

They were admitted alphabetically. Nina came third. The corpulent little Pope sat in a green and gold room frescoed by the Caracci. He smiled at Nina's curtsey, held out his peasant's hand for her kiss, asked if she understood Italian, where she was from, how she liked Rome. It was very beautiful. Very brief. And Nina backed out, yielding to Červa, whose fear-worked sweat glands had already gone to work on her new dress.

When the last girl returned, the Pope waddled out to pose for pictures. He stood beside Sister Angie Caterina, who raised her eyes to his generous chin and babbled what he may have thought English but which the girls knew was the senseless litany of her ecstasy and terror. "We're ready now," said the good Pope to the photographer.

But not quite, for Červa cried out. "Papa, one moment, please."

"Of course, my dear. What is it?"

Červa went over to the sofa and, from under her coat, drew out her violin. "All my life I wished to play for you."

The Pope said that there was nothing in the world that would so delight him.

Červa raised her fiddle arm. Horrific stains released their terrible aroma. Then out of the tortured fiddle struggled Gounod's "Ave Maria," perhaps never in the history of performance played with such passionate deformity. The Pope smiled unremittingly. When Červa's thick arm lowered from its musical slaughter, he said, *"Molto*

141

bello, cara. I am grateful to you." He waved to the photographer, smiled for the flash, and disappeared.

3

The girls returned to the palazzo, stunned, one and all, by the incredible conclusion of the audience.

Sister Clara announced that tonight there would be no permission to leave the house. Since the very concept of permission had been the invention of Clara's fury, it spurred a mass exodus. Nina had the sisters to herself.

Around the dining room table they sat, sweating in their wimples. Sister Angie Caterina still muttered the grim syllables which bound her dim memory to the great occasion. Into this low static, Nina said, "Sisters, I'm going to leave Rome tomorrow."

Sister Louella dropped her coffee cup on the Persian carpet.

"Mother of God," said Sister Mary Pia.

"I cannot do my work here, Sisters. I've got to leave."

Sister Clara rose darkly. "Ingratitude," she said.

"I'm afraid so, Sister. I hope you'll make my apology to the Cardinal."

"Lord God," wailed Sister Angie Caterina, driven to clarity by the word "Cardinal."

Nina went upstairs, locked her door and packed her bags. For the next hour the door was banged, scratched, knocked and implored at. "Please, dearie." "You must." "Young woman, your scholarship." "Give us another try, Ninie dearie."

"No, Sister, what's left of my mind is made up."

Only to Sibyl did Nina open, and that to refuse an offer

to get Eddie to drive her to the station. "I'm back on my own. I better start getting used to it," though that was only part of the reason. It was time to shake loose from nulls.

"I'd go pretty slow with that one, if I were you," she threw to Sibyl. (Though who could be less like Sibyl than Nina Callahan?)

In any case, it didn't matter. For Nina Callahan, it didn't matter who played *with* or who played *for* anyone else at all in this megalomaniacal city of nulls and caesars.

Dr. Cahn's Visit

"How far is it now, George?"

The old man is riding next to his son, Will. George was his brother, dead the day after Franklin Roosevelt. "Almost there, Dad."

"What does 'almost' mean?"

"It's Eighty-Sixth and Park. The hospital's at Ninety-ninth and Fifth. Mother's in the Klingenstein Pavilion."

"Mother's not well?"

"No, she's not well. Liss and I took her to the hospital a couple of weeks ago."

"It must have slipped my mind." The green eyes darkened with sympathy. "I'm sure you did the right thing. Is it a good hospital?"

"Very good. You were on staff there half a century."

"Of course I was. For many years, I believe."

"Fifty."

"Many as that."

"A little slower, pal. These jolts are hard on the old man."

The cabbie was no chicken himself. "It's your ride."

"Are we nearly there, George?"

"Two minutes more."

"The day isn't friendly," said Dr. Cahn. "I don't remember such—such—"

"Heat."

"Heat in New York." He took off his gray fedora and scratched at the hairless, liver-spotted skin. Circulatory difficulty left it dry, itchy. Scratching had shredded and inflamed its soft center.

"It's damn hot. In the nineties. Like you."

"What's that?"

"It's as hot as you are old. Ninety-one."

"Ninety-one. That's not good."

"It's a grand age."

"That's your view."

"And mother's eighty. You've lived good, long lives."

"Mother's not well, son?"

"Not too well. That's why Liss and I thought you ought to see her. Mother's looking forward to seeing you."

"Of course. I should be with her. Is this the first time I've come to visit?"

"Yes."

"I should be with her."

The last weeks at home had been difficult. Dr. Cahn had been the center of the household. Suddenly, his wife was. The nurses looked after her. And when he talked, she didn't answer. He grew angry, sullen. When her ulcerous mouth improved, her voice was rough and her thought

146

harsh. "I wish you'd stop smoking for five minutes. Look at the ashes on your coat. Please stop smoking."

"Of course, dear. I didn't know I was annoying you." The ash tumbled like a suicide from thirty stories, the butt was crushed into its dead brothers. "I'll smoke inside." And he was off, but, in two minutes, back. Lighting up. Sometimes he lit two cigarettes at once. Or lit the filtered end. The odor was foul, and sometimes his wife was too weak to register her disgust.

They sat and lay within silent yards of each other. Dr. Cahn was in his favorite armchair, the *Times* bridge column inches from his cigarette. He read it all day long. The vocabulary of the game deformed his speech. "I need some clubs" might mean "I'm hungry." "My spades are tired" meant he was. Or his eyes were. Praise of someone might come out "He laid his hand out clearly." In the bedridden weeks, such mistakes intensified his wife's exasperation. "He's become such a penny-pincher," she said to Liss when Dr. Cahn refused to pay her for the carton of cigarettes she brought, saying, "They can't charge so much. You've been cheated."

"Liss has paid. Give her the money."

"Are you telling me what's trump? I've played this game all my life."

"You certainly have. And I can't bear it."

In sixty marital years, there had never been such anger. When Will came from Chicago to persuade his mother into the hospital, the bitterness dismayed him.

It was, therefore, not so clear that Dr. Cahn should visit his wife. Why disturb her last days? Besides, Dr. Cahn seldom went out anywhere. He wouldn't walk with the black nurses (women whom he loved, teased and was teased by). It wasn't done. "I'll go out later. My feet aren't friendly today." Or, lowering the paper, "My legs can't trump."

Liss opposed his visit. "Mother's afraid he'll make a scene."

"It doesn't matter," said Will. "He has to have some sense of what's happening. They've been the center of each other's lives. It wouldn't be right."

The hope had been that Dr. Cahn would die first. He was ten years older, his mind had slipped its moorings years ago. Mrs. Cahn was clearheaded, and, except near the end, energetic. She loved to travel, wanted especially to visit Will in Chicago—she'd not seen his new apartment— but she wouldn't leave her husband even for a day. "Suppose something happened."

"Bring him along."

"He can't travel. He'd make an awful scene."

Only old friends tolerated him, played bridge with him, forgiving his lapses and muddled critiques of their play. "If you don't understand a two bid now, you never will." The most gentlemanly of men, Dr. Cahn's tongue roughened with his memory. It was as if a lifetime of restraint were only the rind of a wicked impatience.

"He's so spoiled," said Mrs. Cahn, the spoiler.

"Here we are, Dad."

They parked under the blue awning. Dr. Cahn got out his wallet—he always paid for taxis, meals, shows—looked at the few bills, then handed it to his son. Will took a dollar, added two of his own and thanked his father.

"This is a weak elevator," he said of one of the monsters made to drift the ill from floor to floor. A nurse wheeled in a stretcher and Dr. Cahn removed his fedora.

"Mother's on Eight."

148

Dr. Cahn's Visit

"Minnie is here?"

"Yes. She's ill. Step out now."

"I don't need your hand."

Each day, his mother filled less of the bed. Her face, unsupported by dentures, seemed shot away. Asleep, it looked to Will as if the universe leaned on the crumpled cheeks. When he kissed them, he feared they'd turn to dust, so astonishingly delicate was the flesh. The only vanity left was love of attention, and that was part of the only thing that counted, the thought of those who cared for her. How she appreciated the good nurses, and her children. They—who'd never before seen their mother's naked body—would change her nightgown if the nurse were gone. They brought her the bedpan, and, though she usually suggested they leave the room, sat beside her while, under the sheets, her weak body emptied its small waste.

For the first time in his adult life, Will found her beautiful. Her flesh was mottled like a Pollock canvas, the facial skin trenched with the awful last ditches of self-defense; but her look melted him. It was human beauty.

Day by day, manners that seemed as much a part of her as her eyes—fussiness, bossiness, nagging inquisitiveness—dropped away. She was down to what she was.

Not since childhood had she held him so closely, kissed his cheek with such force. "This is mine. This is what lasts," said the force.

What was she to him? Sometimes, little more than the old organic scenery of his life. Sometimes she was the meaning of it. "Hello, darling," she'd say. "I'm so glad to see you." The voice, never melodious, was rusty, avian. Beautiful. No actress could match it. "How are you? What's happening?"

"Very little. How are you today?"

149

She told her news. "Dr. Vacarian was in, he wanted to give me another treatment. I told him, 'No more.' And no more medicine." Each day she'd renounced more therapy. An unspoken decision had been made after a five hour barium treatment which usurped the last of her strength. (Will thought that might have been its point.) It had given her her last moments of eloquence, a frightening jeremiad about life dark beyond belief, nothing left, nothing right. It was the last complaint of an old champion of complaint, and after it, she'd made up her mind to go. There was no more talk of going home.

"Hello, darling. How are you today?"

Will bent over, was kissed and held against her cheek. "Mother, Dad's here."

To his delight, she showed hers. "Where is he?" Dr. Cahn had waited at the door. Now he came in, looked at the bed, realized where he was and who was there.

"Dolph, dear. How are you, my darling? I'm so happy you came to see me."

The old man stooped over and took her face in his hands. For seconds, there was silence. "My dearest," he said; then, "I didn't know. I had no idea. I've been so worried about you. But don't worry now. You look wonderful. A little thin, perhaps. We'll fix that. We'll have you out in no time."

The old man's pounding heart must have driven blood through the clogged vessels. There was no talk of trumps.

"You can kiss me, dear." Dr. Cahn put his lips on hers.

He sat next to the bed and held his wife's hand through the low rail. Over and over he told her she'd be fine. She asked about home and the nurses. He answered well for a while. Then they both saw him grow vague and tired. To

150

Dr. Cahn's Visit

Will he said, "I don't like the way she's looking. Are you sure she has a good doctor?"

Of course Mrs. Cahn heard. Her happiness watered a bit, not at the facts, but at his inattention. Still, she held on. She knew he could not sit so long in a strange room. "I'm so glad you came, darling."

Dr. Cahn heard his cue and rose. "We mustn't tire you, Minnie dear. We'll come back soon."

She held out her small arms, he managed to lean over, and they kissed again.

In the taxi, he was very tired. "Are we home?"

"Almost, Dad. You're happy you saw mother, aren't you?"

"Of course I'm happy. But it's not a good day. It's a very poor day. Not a good bid at all."